Copyright @2021 by Austin Chukwuemeka Konkwo

This publication contains the opinions and ideas of its author. It is intended to provide helpful and informative material on the subjects addressed in the publication. The author and publisher specifically disclaim all responsibility for any liability, loss or risk, personal or otherwise, which is incurred as a consequence, directly or indirectly, of the use and application of any of the contents of this book.

WORKBOOK PRESS LLC
187 E Warm Springs Rd,
Suite B285, Las Vegas, NV 89119, USA

Website: https://workbookpress.com/
Hotline: 1-888-818-4856
Email: admin@workbookpress.com

Ordering Information:
Quantity sales. Special discounts are available on quantity purchases by corporations, associations, and others. For details, contact the publisher at the address above.

ISBN-13:   978-1-957618-66-1 (Paperback Version)
                978-1-957618-67-1 (Digital Version)

REV. DATE: 29/12/2022

The Great Impact

By

AUSTIN CHUKWUEMEKA KONKWO

Table Of Contents

FOREWORD

The poor start of Fabian and Nelson can be attributed to intimidation by their school peers and the large part of the blame goes to the weaknesses of the two students. To a great extent, the fault lies at the doorsteps of both parents whose attitude to their children's training can be described as careless. This is because they knew that their children were wayward, resulting into poor academic performance, yet they did nothing to effect a change. They allowed the boys to grow wings, to the extent of renting apartments and stealing. The school shares from the blame. It is very obvious that there is laxity in the school administration, such that students in the boarding house could have rented apartment in town. Although, the general belief is that prison is a training ground for would be criminals, the two boys' lives became transformed there. This brings to the fore, once again, the fact that the two boys changed for the better when both parents and the society (religious organization) took charge. This approves that the misdemeanour in the lives of our youths are actually 'a call' for help and it will be better if all the stakeholders rise to the challenge and make a positive change.

Professor Helen Bodunde

Department of General and Natural Sciences,

Federal University of Agriculture, Abeokuta,

Ogun State, Nigeria.

CHAPTER ONE

While at the primary school, Nelson often felt inferior before some of those in institutions higher than his. He at times saw them from a different perspective; as first class citizens who are sophisticated, impressive, with overwhelming influence and with a lot to offer. He saw some of them as extra-ordinary human beings quite incomparable to himself. Nelson sees some of them as special high breed of people who enjoy a high standard of living and who are more important than him. He always prayed to see himself within the four walls of the secondary school at the shortest possible time as a student.

When Nelson got to the final class of the primary school, he worked harder than he had done before in preparation for the secondary school entrance examination in order to pass. During the entrance examination, Nelson wrote with determination and interest. He had left no stones unturned, during the preparations. Thus, the examination did not pose much problems to him.

After writing the examination, Nelson was very confident of passing the secondary school entrance examination. He wished that the days before the secondary schools are to re-open could reduce from twenty-four hours a day to about twelve if not less, so that he can enroll for secondary school education.

When the results came out, Nelson performed excellently and was given his deserved chance. He prepared with all that the school required in the admission prospectus and left for the school on the re-opening day.

On the first day at school, Nelson was harassed by some students of Lawson Grammar School where he was given admission. They called Nelson abusive names and embarrassed him in a number of ways. The embarrassment was so much that Nelson could not stand on his feet very well throughout the first day of his registration and enrolment. His bitter experience with the students on his first day at school made him to feel more inferior than the other students. He carried other students on a high esteem with utmost respect and fear.

When Nelson finally got to the hostel, he still did not associate very well with the other students. He still looked at them as lords who are quite different from other creatures. Many of the older students did not accommodate Nelson either. Instead, they kept shunning him and in addition rained abuses on him. They called him funny names like toad, fresher among others

Nelson, however, had some relief while mixing with other new students. That was where he actually belonged. The new students on their part accommodated Nelson who was part and parcel of them as "birds of the same feather flock together".

Some other things that made Nelson feel inferior before the older students was due to the way some of the older students spoke and behaved. Most of them had changed their speaking habits in a manner that ordinarily they could be regarded as extra-ordinary human beings. Socially, some people could see them as having acquired some Western culture. Most of them spoke in slangs and pidgin and used vocabularies that were best known to them or some of those already within the school. With all those attributes in some of the already existing students, Nelson considered himself inferior before many other students. Nelson, on his part, was determined to bridge the gap he envisaged was existing between him and the other students. He was bent on covering the gap no matter what it take.

Nelson believed that nothing will stop him from behaving the way most older students were doing. He took that as a challenge and as a task that must be realised in the school. To start with, he had on his own been buying some of the wears which he perceived were popular among many older students. Such ranged from caps, canvasses, T-shirts, bleached jean trousers, styled belts, striped shirts, travelling bags among others. In fact, Nelson was determined to belong to a certain high class of students and nothing can stop him.

The roommate and neighbour to Nelson was Fabian who was in the second year in their school. He was a flamboyant and reckless student. He was like some other students who behaved boyishly. Fabian's behaviour, slangs, intonations and dressings were like those of some other students whom Nelson loved to follow their foot-steps. They were of peculiar character of uncontrolled adolescents, often crazy in utterances and crafty at times. A lifestyle that lays emphasis on the discussion of girls, parties and dances and always watchful of the latest fashion among youths. That was the type of life obtainable among some of the boys in the school then.

Nelson saw Fabian as possessing those qualities he wants to pick up. "Charity begins at home", so people say. To achieve his aim, Nelson resolved to associate with Fabian, his corner mate and neighbor, to reach out to others of similar character.

Some days after Nelson came to know Fabian, Fabian received an invitation for a party organised by Joel, a classmate to Fabian. The invitation letter to Fabian was addressed to Mr. & Mrs. Fabian. Fabian wanted to attend the party with Nelson instead of a lady even though it was explicitly stated that every man should attend with a lady, while a lady is to attend with one man. It was indicated on the card thus "one man one woman show".

As soon as Fabian told Nelson of the party and that he should go along with him, Nelson shouted "oh! goodness, a party; I will surely go". The party was fixed for 6:00 p.m. the following evening. Fabian informed Nelson to get set on or before the time. Nelson promised to get ready for the party before the scheduled time.

That day, Nelson who was desirous of the party was set before the scheduled time. He dressed up for the party in a good attire around 5:00 p.m. in readiness for the schedule time. He kept on reminding Fabian of the party and its scheduled time. That was the first time Nelson was to attend a party since he came into the school.

When Fabian got set for the party, both left and got to the venue of the party at about 6:00 p.m. Not many people had come to the party then and some of those already at the hall were dancing. Nelson and Fabian went into the hall and started dancing along with many others. Later, a friend to Fabian, by name Johnson, asked Fabian about the lady that he came with Fabian pointed at Nelson. Fabian told Johnson that "in the absence of a she a he can do the job of a she and that in the absence of a woman, a man can do the work of a woman". Johnson burst into laughter and in refuting the claim said "not at all, a he is a he and a she is a she anywhere".

Later, people were asked to leave the hall to enable only those invited for the party to come in. The master of the ceremony and the organiser explicitly said "on no account should any uninvited person come near the party hall. Every invited man will only be allowed into the hall if he is with a girl while any invited girl will only be allowed into the hall if she is with a man. People without partners will not be allowed in. My statements are irrevocable".

Those who had all the requirements moved into the party hall leaving behind those that did not have the stated requirements. With those requirements, Nelson and Fabian were not qualified to enter into the dancing hall. However, they tried to enter the hall but were not allowed by those manning the gate of the hall called "bouncers". The boys felt infuriated and went back to their school .

On their way back to school, Nelson asked Fabian what it takes to organise a party. Fabian informed Nelson of what it could take to organise a party based on the party he (Fabian) organized sometime ago. Fabian said that it could take about four Dinab to organise a party. Nelson on that spot gave Fabian four Dinab to organise a party for him. Nelson said to Fabian "organise a free for all party for me, as soon as we get to the school".

At school, Fabian circulated invitation cards to people for a party in two days time. Fabian prepared seriously for the party which he tagged "class jump":

On the day of the party, many people honoured the invitation including Johnson. While Johnson was dancing with others at the party, Nelson came to him and pushed him out of the dancing hall without telling him the reason. Nelson succeeded in humiliating Johnson back. Nelson also used that singular party to inform people within the school that he has arrived.

As time went on, the friendship between Nelson and

Fabian became intimate. To keep their friendship, Nelson allowed Fabian to take advantage of their relationship by exploiting him. That was Nelson's effort towards consolidating his friendship with Fabian. It is believed that "to have a friend close one eye, to keep a friend close two".

Nelson allowed Fabian to take advantage of him in many ways. Such included Fabian's acts of collecting Nelson's beverages, detergents, foodstuffs and so on for his personal use. However, Nelson allowed that with caution because it is believed that "one cannot use what is meant for one to pay another otherwise it might not be kindness again but rather foolishness".

Fabian had on his own observed what Nelson wanted and had taken his time to teach Nelson how to achieve his aim in social circle. As time went on, both boys became perfect match and inseparable. They could attend clubs, social gatherings, tours, outside school sports activities and other engagements together. At that first year of Nelson's admission, he had started engaging in activities more than Fabian his mentor. Nelson was absenting himself from classes a lot, even though records of attendance were always taken.

Nelson on his own nicknamed himself "Nelson guy".

That was in line with funny names which many students took to. The name "Nelson guy" will attract Nelson's attention. Fabian within that time had taken Nelson to many outside social engagements apart from those obtainable at Lawson Grammar

School. Nelson who was desirous to belong to the powerful social class quickly picked-up. At a certain time, he started to attend more social engagements apart from those that was obtainable at the school and also apart from those Fabian was taking him along with.

One cannot serve two masters effectively at the same time, so people say. Nelson was at a point giving more priority to social activities than his academic work. That led to his failure during the first term of his first year in his school. He had the twenty ninth position in his class of thirty students. His failure came into being because he had asked for it. He had spent more time in his school smoking, attending outside dances and sleeping outside the school premises than devoting attention to studies.

Nelson's first term result was dispatched to his parents in accordance with the school rules and regulations. In his result and assessment report card, his conduct was indicated as unsatisfactory and it was stated that he was a truant, at school and insubordinate to authorities.

CHAPTER TWO

While Nelson was spending his first term holiday at home, his first term result was received. When his parents went through the result, they were highly annoyed. They called on Nelson and queried him over his poor performance. Nelson attributed the poor result to intimidation from the teachers in his school, whom he claimed hated and victimized him so much for no just reason. He even claimed that some teachers had requested for bribes from him to pass him but that he never obliged them. Nelson said that such was criminal and therefore he always refused.

Hearing all that, Nelson's parents were bittered. They were also poised for action to revenge those who had caused their son's failure. They resolved to deal mercilessly with the concerned teachers. They immediately scheduled to visit Lawson Grammar School the following day to find out why some teachers collaborated to deal with their son, an anticipated honest individual.

However, Nelson's parents expressed doubt on his allegations. They wondered how all the teachers could collectively victimise a single student. But they had seen and observed Nelson over the years, in fact, from his childhood as someone that is eager to learn, respectful, hardworking, dedicated to whatever assignment that had been given to him and above all intelligent. So, the whole issue was difficult to reconcile.

They wondered if Nelson had changed over a very short time of the first term. They could not believe that for a number of reasons. For one thing, Nelson had behaved well since he returned for the holidays. That had marred the chances of anyone thinking that he had been bad at school. He had been showing those good qualities which he had been known for at their home before he left for Lawson Grammar School.

Secondly, the period of Nelson's stay for the first term was so short that no one could think that a serious change could have erupted for bad. The period of the first term was about three months.

Thirdly, Nelson was religious before he left for the boarding school. When he came back for the holidays, he was still showing that same manner of religious life and up-bringing. His parents had examined likely reasons for his failure and predicaments but could not find. They therefore concluded that the alleged victimization by the teachers could be a reality.

A plan on how to visit Lawson Grammar School and deal ruthlessly with the concerned teachers immediately was arrived at. They concluded to visit the school the following day with some Police Intelligence Officers who should be in mofty. The District Police Officer was contacted immediately and he agreed to give his men who will escort Nelson's parents to the school. The District Police Officer also accepted that the Police Intelligence Officers who should undertake the assignment should be in mofty to make investigations and detections easy.

The following day, Nelson's parents asked him to prepare so that they could all go to Lawson Grammar School. Nelson felt very reluctant to go to the school with his parents. He knew that he had lied to his parents with regards to the cause of his failure at the examinations. Nelson complained that he was sick and as such cannot undertake the journey.

Nelson's parent insisted that in view of the sensitive nature of the matter, he should go with them. They informed Nelson that they would take him to a medical practitioner for treatment as soon as they come back from the journey. Nelson insisted that he would not undertake the journey with them. He kept giving one flimsy excuse or the other to backup his stand.

After all said and done, Nelson did not agree to go to Lawson Grammar School with his parents. He went inside his room, lied on his bed and covered himself with wrapper pretending to be sick. He started shedding crocodile tears as if he was dying. His parents also concluded that Nelson's sudden sickness must have resulted from the shock of the poor performance in the examination; and the victimization he had suffered from his teachers.

The following morning, Nelson's parents set off to Lawson Grammar School. They left their home to pick up the Police Officers for the journey. They had considered the crucial nature of the matter and never wanted to take chances. In fact, the manner and way in which they left for the investigation showed that they were poised for action and were determined to withstand any likely confrontation that could erupt while executing their vengeance plans. They were even ready for any physical assault, if necessary, on any teacher who had deliberately failed Nelson or was in any way instrumental to Nelson's failure.

When they arrived at the police station, they made statements before they drove to Lawson Grammar School. Nelson's parents discussed with the policemen accompanying them. The policemen equally condemned the acts by some teachers which had adversely effected the well being of some innocent students through various forms of victimization for one selfish reason or the other.

The Police Officers stressed bitterly on such and vehemently condemned it. They mentioned that some teachers had in the processes of victimization ruined the lives of many innocent students. They emphasized that if such acts are not put to a stop, the educational system would be messed up and failures and passes among students would be at the mercy of teachers and not on merit. They claimed that in some cases, students who had passed very well in examinations had been marked down by teachers for selfish reasons while some students who had failed woefully had emerged successful as a result of the inordinate and baseless attitudes of some teachers in apportioning rewards.

Hearing all that, Nelson's parents who were well-to-do financially and highly placed in status as top government officers became more aggrieved and were poised to deal mercilessly with any teacher who had failed Nelson unjustly, at least to act as a deterrant to other erring teachers. While inside their car, they resolved to return war for war, fire for fire and even thuggery for thuggery to any culprit if the need arises.

However, the society was not very sound morally and socially. The society did not give much room for excellence from the citizens. The society embraced capitalism and the citizens became egocentric hence there was materialism and decay. All that paved way to mediocricy, favoritism and frustrations.

CHAPTER THREE

On getting to Lawson Grammar School, Nelson's parents went to the Principal of the school. The security men gave them and the Police Intelligence Officers access at both the school gate and at the Principal's office, without following protocols because Nelson's parents were top government functionaries and friends of the Principal.

At the reception in the Principal's office, a teacher came to Nelson's parents and greeted them. The teacher had known Nelson's parents before then even though Nelson's parents did not know him. The teacher introduced himself as Mr. Clement Parrow and that he was Nelson's History teacher.

As soon as the teacher mentioned that he was a teacher to Nelson, Nelson's father who had been annoyed nearly abused the teacher. Nelson's father, Mr. Johnson Kenneth, saw Mr. Clement Parrow as an enemy who needed to be attacked on the spot. Mr. Kenneth asked the Police Officers to abuse the teacher but the Police Officers refused but rather calmed Mr. Kenneth down at that moment. Mr. Johnson Kenneth later restrained his confrontational behaviour as an educated person. He thereafter ignored Mr. Clement Parrow and turned his back on him.

Nelson's father was still full of bitterness. In addition, he uttered an abusive statement by saying "teachers are these days abusive, money conscious, wicked and disgruntled". Mr. Parrow felt embarrassed over the treatment and left the place.

Later, Mr. Johnson Kenneth, his wife and the Police Officers were ushered into the Principal's office. The Principal seeing Mr. Kenneth and his entourage, stood up, shook hands with each of them and gave them seats. Mr. Samuel Dowin, the school Principal thanked Mr. Johnson Kenneth for finding time to visit him in the company of his wife and others.

Without allowing Mr. Kenneth to talk, Mr. Dowin started talking of Nelson's attitude at school. He complained that Nelson was fond of absenting himself from school and classes; smokes and also attends irrelevant engagements outside the school premises, attributing that to the cause of his failure at the first term examinations. He further stressed that Nelson was always associating with men and students of questionable character and imitating their lifestyle thereby causing harm to himself. Mr. Dowin said that failure was normal because according to him "a goat that does not chew cud could start chewing the cud if it associates with the goat that chews the cud".

Mr. Dowin expressed dissatisfaction over Nelson's recent character which he stated as bad and disappointing. He mentioned that Nelson was a good and well behaved student when he enrolled into the school but stated that the sudden change was unfortunate. Mr. Dowin further brought out the class attendance register for those in first year and showed to Mr. Johnson Kenneth. There, Mr. Kenneth saw with his eyes that Nelson was a truant, having not met up to forty percent of attendance in subjects.

Mr. Dowin mentioned that with such poor record of attendance, the school was so kind to have allowed Nelson to write his examinations. He claimed that the school could not have allowed Nelson to sit for that first term examinations because he did not satisfy the minimum attendance requirement of at least sixty percent of the total period of teaching time for every subject to enable one write an examination in any subject. He said that the school decided to set aside that rule, that term on humanitarian grounds.

The principal further said that Nelson's character was nothing to write home about. He claimed that Nelson hardly read his books and never took his studies seriously. He expressed dissatisfaction on how Mr. Kenneth, a highly respected

Senior Officer in the government could have a child whose character is poor and below expectation. Mr. Dowin advised Mr. Kenneth to caution Nelson at home, advise him to turn a new leaf and change his present ways of life for the better. He warned that if Nelson does not change for the school will have no option than to expel him from the school because the school does not accommodate waywardness and carefree attitudes.

To further back up his points, the Principal invited Nelson's Form Master and Hostel Master to address Nelson's parents. The two people came to the Principal after a short while. The two teachers also complained of Nelson's non-challant attitude to work and poor behaviour at the school. They all advised Mr. Kenneth to warn Nelson to desist from reckless and carefree attitude to studies. The Hostel Master showed Mr. Kenneth the register of students that slept at their hostel on a daily basis. At the register, Nelson did not sleep at the hostel for so many times while his whereabouts were not made known to the authority. The class teacher also showed Mr. Kenneth his own copy of students' attendance to lessons. At the register, it was noticed before all present including Mr. and Mrs. Kenneth that Nelson was a truant. The form teacher further said that Nelson engaged in so many illegal and illicit social engagements outside the school premises. With the enumerated points, it was clear before Nelson's parents and the police detectives that Nelson was carefree to studies, non-challant to work, a truant and was behaving poorly at the school.

Nelson's parents .and the police detectives thanked the principal and other staff of the school for the wonderful information they had given them They promised to discharge their duties accordingly in advising Nelson to be of good behaviour and also to be hardworking at school. All parties thanked the other for the second time before departing the Principal's office.

At that point, Nelson's father, Mr. Johnson Kenneth, felt so sorry for what he had done to Mr. Clement Parrow. Mr. Kenneth immediately sent some people to call Mr. Parrow for him to enable him apologise to him for his behavior towards him.

Those sent told Mr. Clement Parrow that somebody called Mr. Johnson Kenneth want to see him. Mr. Parrow thinking that more abuses was on the line for him, refused to honour the invitation. After waiting for so long but could not see Mr. Parrow, Mr. Kenneth asked where he could locate Mr. Parrow. He was taken to Mr. Parrow's office by a school staff.

Mr. Kenneth and his entourage met Mr. Parrow. They apologized to him for the insults and abuses rained on him. Mr. Parrow accepted the apology but told Mr. and Mrs Kenneth to advise Nelson to be hardworking, attentive to classes, honest, reliable and dedicated to studies. He mentioned that Nelson's attitude to work was poor

Mr. and Mrs. Kenneth gave Mr. Parrow one Dinab as a mark of their appreciation for what he had told them and for the insult rendered on him. Mr.Parrow refused to accept the money as such was the culture. Thereafter, Mr. Kenneth and members of his entourage left for home.

CHAPTER FOUR

On their way home, the police detectives advised Mr. Kenneth to always examine matters thoroughly before laying blames on people. They mentioned that if Mr. Kenneth had embarked on any remarkable assault on any remarkable assault on any member of the school authority, they would have had it rough since assault is an offence punishable by law. They advised Mr. Johnson Kenneth to always examine people's allegations and claims on other people before taking any measure or action against the accused. They said that if that is not done, one is bound to take up actions which the person could later regret and in addition the law will have the offender punished. Mr. Kenneth noted and bore that in his mind. Mr. Kenneth dropped the two police detectives at the police station and drove to his house.

At their home, Nelson's parents called on Nelson and asked him of his conduct at school. Nelson said that his conduct was satisfactory. His parents refuted his claim and warned him to denounce his poor behaviour at school and turn a new leaf for his own good and for the good of their family.

Nelson knew that what his parents were saying were right and therefore was relieved. His parents too were talking with facts and therefore did not accept the excuses which Nelson was using to camouflage. They warned him sternly and stated that if that continues, they would have him severely punished.

For the greater period of the discussion and advises, Nelson was calm and sober. He showed remorse on what he had done and what he failed to do. Nelson pleaded for pardon for his misdeamanour. He said that he would never repeat any lapses noticed of him again. He however stressed that his failure could be attributed to himself somehow and attributed to teachers and the school authorities too. He promised to makeup any shortfalls on his part at the next terminal examination.

Thereafter, Nelson's mother told him of the usefulness of education. She mentioned that the benefits range from enhancement in social status, recognition, acceptance to enlightenment and the ability to get better and well paid jobs. Within that time, the sickness which Nelson claimed he was having when his parents wanted to take him to Lawson Grammar School vanished as he was seen behaving healthy again.

It must be noted that Nelson was pretending to be sick in order not to go with his parents to his school. That was actually a mere pretence and not sickness

When Nelson's parents observed that Nelson had shown some good signs of remorse, they left him. Mr. Kenneth had wanted to beat-up Nelson as a way of cautioning him but had abandoned such idea since he did not know whether Nelson was actually sick or not. Nelson knew that he could be flogged if it was eventually discovered that he was not doing his work very well at school. He avoided punishment under the guise of being sick.

Nelson's parents, resolved to be advising him regularly to be of good behaviour at school and at other places. They also agreed to reduce his pocket money at school. They thought that his reckless behaviour at school was because he had the money to embark on such extravagances. They further concluded to adjust their relationship, kindness and the act of pampering him to see whether that could encourage maturity and good conduct on his part.

His parents also planned to arrange extra classes for him. They contacted some teachers whom they paid reasonable sums of money to teach him at home for the remaining part of the holidays.

CHAPTER FIVE

Nelson concluded that nothing will stop him from engaging and partaking in most social engagements at school no matter the measures used to deter him. He was bent on achieving his social desires and needs.

The contacted teachers during that holiday kept coming to give Nelson lectures, but Nelson had a divided attention on the lectures because he was spending most of his time thinking about social engagements at school. Therefore, he paid less attention to the lectures and as such derived little out of them. That was one of the efforts geared towards ensuring that Nelson excelled academically.

When first term holiday ended, Nelson arranged to go back to school. Before he was taken to school, he was given some words of advice and encouragement. He was advised to be of good behaviour, to be hardworking, dedicated to studies and law abiding to the school rules and regulations. His parents, friends and relations all advised him.

Despite all the advices, Nelson still resolved to live the life he wanted to live at school. When he met Fabian at school, he narrated his experiences. He informed Fabian that when his parents received his result in which he failed, they were angry. He mentioned that he told his parents that it was teachers' victimization that made him to fail. He said further that his parents were annoyed after hearing all that and therefore wanted to find out the authenticity of his statements. He further said that his parents went to their school in the company of some Police Intelligence Officers and found out that he was telling lies and thereafter warned him after all efforts to beat him up failed because he claimed that he was sick. He told Fabian that his parents organised extra classes for him to enable him acquire more educational knowledge apart from that which he was meant to receive at school. He said that his parents were so much interested in seeing him prosper academically and are ready to sacrifice anything to make him realise that goal.

Replying, Fabian said "enjoyment is one thing and education is another thing. None can be compromised for the other. We are youths and enjoyment to us at this our time cannot be compromised for another thing at all. Enjoyment will take care of every other thing. One is bound to have more friends, more fun, dances, prices and so on from engaging in series of social engagements. Nelson's parents had their own fair share of the series of enjoyment in life and now want to deny Nelson who is a young breed his own portion. Life is in stages. If one does not have his own share of what a young man is meant to have, the person cannot have such an opportunity again. The old cannot engage in the young people's affairs just as the young ones cannot undertake the old people's activities. Do not be deterred by the old people and their words".

Nelson said "I have ignored all that my parents said. Nothing can be compromised for my youth life for youth life is once in a life time".

As the school session went on, Nelson was seen with Fabian engaging in several social engagements both within and outside the school premises. Two of them enrolled into the membership of more than sixty percent of the social clubs in the school. None was a religious association. They changed their names to "boy Nel" and "boy Fab". Any word "boy Nel"and "boy Fab" will definitely attract Nelson's or Fabian's attention respectively. In addition to those social engagements, both were chain cigarette smokers, drunkards and women addicts. To further boost their ruggedness, the boys wore bleached and worn out jean trousers, painted T-shirts, styled caps and big canvass most of the time. In fact, Nelson and Fabian paid very little attention to studies and more attention to social engagements.

Two weeks after the re-opening of the school, Nelson's form teacher saw Nelson and Fabian in the school compound at a hideout at odd hour looking confused. The teacher called Nelson and Fabian. There, the teacher advised the boys to be of good behavior so that they will not run into problems that might put them in difficulties. When the boys came out from the teacher's office, Fabian told Nelson that "if everybody is law abiding, the policemen and members of the security forces may not be employed since there won't be need for their employment and remuneration. Prison is meant for human beings and not spirits. It is because prisons are existing that made the governments to engage people as warders. The boys laughed over the teacher's advice on their way.

CHAPTER SIX

For Nelson, right from his childhood, he was used to living a descent and comfortable life. He was born with silver spoons in his mouth. So, it was difficult for him to reverse the trend.

With the reduction in his pocket money, Nelson could not meet with his social needs any longer. Nelson's parents had earlier warned him not to be coming home to demand for money unless there was need for that. He was fed very well at school and all his books for the year were bought for him by his father. Also, the pocket money given to him when he was sent back to school was enough ordinarily to sustain him. His parents never made much provision to accommodate extravagances and trivialities.

The money given to Nelson as time went on could not enable him to take proper care of his numerous social engagements. But on his part, he was determined to engage in most of the activities. He has taken them as routine activities and as a task that must be accomplished.

When he highlighted his financial predicaments to Fabian, Fabian told him to go to his parents and fake a story to draw sympathy from them. Fabian told Nelson to tell Mr. and Mrs. Kenneth that he has broken an amoeba, a costly and very important scientific equipment at school and that if he does not replace the amoeba he will be expelled from the school. But Fabian asked Nelson whether Mr. and Mrs. Kenneth were educated in science so as to know that amoeba cannot be broken.

Nelson told Fabian that his father did not study science and may not know much in sciences. Fabian therefore concluded that the affair could work since Mr. Kenneth does not know much about sciences. Further, Fabian told Nelson to be frowning and crying while narrating his predicaments so that he would be taken serious. Nelson arranged to meet his parents the following day.

The following morning, Nelson told his hall warden that he was sick and want to go home. Nelson told the warden that his sickness was severe and defies the first aid treatment obtainable at the hostel. The hostel warden granted Nelson's request to go home. Nelson, that same day, left for his home. Fabian also left for his own home promising to execute the same act and get some money from his parents too.

At home, Nelson was warmly received by his mother. He was further thrilled with good dishes at home. Nelson, almost weeping, told his mother that he had broken amoeba at their school laboratory and that the school has decided to expel him if he does not replace the broken material immediately. He said that the school gave him only a day to bring the money equivalent to the cost of the amoeba or be expelled from the school. After the narrations, Nelson wept more to the extent that his mother became so worried and started to calm him down. She asked Nelson the amount to be used to replace the broken amoeba. He told his mother that two Dinab was involved to replace the material. Nelson's mother who knew that her son has an unrosy and unappealing relationship with the school authorities was afraid. She wondered what could happen to Nelson if he fails to replace the amoeba on or before the given time.

Without wasting time, Nelson's mother ran inside her room. As Nelson's mother ran inside her room, Nelson knew that his mother had gone to bring the requested money. Nelson, a Christian who has not attended church services for a long time knelt down to thank God. When Mrs. Kenneth came out from her room with the two Dinab, she gave same to Nelson and asked him to run straight to the school and pay the required money to replace the broken material. She in addition gave him one

Dinab as pocket money. The woman further advised Nelson to continue to be of good behaviour; work hard and remain law abiding to the school rules and regulations.

As soon as Nelson left home, he smiled and thanked God for a successful outing. That was how he used gimmick to perpetuate evil.

Nelson ran as fast as he could to school. When he met Fabian, he narrated to him how he successfully executed their plan and succeeded. Fabian responding said "whoever is not clever in life is bound to loose since the world is dynamic giving no room to anyone that does not move on the same pace with it".

Fabian said that on his own he has done far more greater things in life compared to what had been done. He mentioned that "for people who live above their income or for students who live above the standard expected of students has something instrumental to that".

Both Fabian and Nelson came to school with a huge sum of money as a result of deceit. Fabian did exactly what Nelson did and extorted a huge sum of money from his parents too. Both after narrating to one another how they went about their plans congratulated one another for a job well done. Fabian got one Dinab from his parents.

With the numerous social engagements Nelson and Fabian were into, the money they collected did not go any way in meeting their social engagements. After a little while, the money they collected got exhausted.

When the money Nelson and Fabian collected finished completely, both thought of a way of getting more money from their parents. They had a discussion on that and finally came up with a plan. They resolved to meet their respective parents with a list of textbooks which are non existent. They resolved to meet their parents with those non-existent textbooks and inform their parents that the purchase of such books is a prerequisite to passing their examinations.

They resolved to tell their parents that the books are obtainable only at their school bookshop. But they realised that if they should say that the books are only obtainable at their school, their parents could suspect foul on their part as a book could be seen at other places. They saw the idea that if they should say that the books are obtainable both elsewhere and in their school, their parents could believe them.

Three weeks after extorting money from their parents, Fabian and Nelson arranged to meet their parents again the following day.

The following day, the boys met their hostel warden and informed him that they were sick and would like to go home for medical attention. They claimed that their sickness was such that could defy the first aid treatment obtainable at the school. Their hostel warden granted their travelling request.

Before they left for their homes, both had written out four books which they will claim were seriously needed for their studies. Three of such books were non-existent while one was existent. The lined up non-existing books were:

1) Book of Biology by S.P. Blown

2) Geography for Stone by P.P. Hawkins

3) Sciences for the sky by S.C. Manny

The existent book was:
Science for secondary schools by P.O. Hawlown. It must be noted that the existent book was not required by Nelson and Fabian.

The boys had resolved to add one existent textbook so that the booksellers will not think that those who had listed those books are jokers, should their parents choose to buy the books for them. The boys had examined all available loopholes in their tricks and made provisions to cover them. What they had done was normal because "right thinking people do not reason only in one direction". People always make provision for lapses and loopholes likely to be envisaged in any transaction.

At home, Nelson was received warmly by his parents. His mother gave him food to eat and water to take his bath. Later on, Nelson told his parents about his mission home. He told them that he had come to present to them the books they were asked to buy at school. He said that the books are so important that his having them was a prerequisite towards his success at their examinations. Nelson informed his parents that if they do not want to have a repeat of what happened to him at the last examinations, they should consider buying the books a matter of urgency. Nelson's parents who were desirous of their son's success at the school promised to buy those listed books the following day. They thanked Nelson for considering the reading of his books a priority to other things. They congratulated Nelson for his academic foresight and promised to do their best to enable him attain the height he was desiring to get to.

The following day, Nelson's father, Mr. Johnson Kenneth went to the town to buy the listed books. Mr. Kenneth almost visited all the prominent bookshops at Nolak town but could not see those non existent listed books. It was the forth book that he saw and bought. The booksellers told Mr. Kenneth that they have not come across or heard of the first three listed books before.

Some of the booksellers informed Mr. Kenneth that the first three listed books were non-existent while some told Mr. Kenneth that those books could be newly introduced books which are yet to get to the markets. Mr. Kenneth who had no idea that Nelson could play the trick of listing non-existent books had the impression that the first three listed textbooks were newly introduced books that are yet to get to the bookshops. He only bought the forth book and went home.

At home, Mr. Johnson Kenneth informed Nelson that he could not see the first three listed textbooks at the bookshops. He informed Nelson that some booksellers informed him that those books could be newly introduced books which may not have circulated very well.

Nelson stated that the first three listed books were newly

introduced books that have not circulated very well. He claimed that he had earlier envisaged difficulty on the part of his father in getting those books; stating that the remaining books are new and can only be bought at their school. Mr. Johnson Kenneth asked Nelson how much it could take to buy those books at their school. Nelson said that each of those books costs one Dinab.

Without wasting time Mr. Johnson Kenneth opened his portfolio and brought out three Dinab which he gave to Nelson to enable him buy the listed books at his school. In addition, he gave Nelson two Dinab as his pocket money. Nelson's mother on her own privately gave Nelson one Dinab to enable him sustain himself at school. Nelson left for school with happiness the following day.

Fabian's story was different. His parents had no time to go to the market to buy any book for him. They asked him the amount that could enable him buy the listed books. Fabian informed them that it would cost four Dinab. His parents simply gave him six Dinab to enable him buy the listed books and also have some pocket money at school.

When Nelson and Fabian came back to their school, they narrated to each other how they successfully executed their plan. Each showed the other the money he had realised. Both congratulated the other for a job well done.

As a result of their success in their outing, both changed their nicknames. They chosed to be called and addressed as "Doos". Nelson took after the name "Nelson Doo" while Fabian chosed to be called and addressed as "Fab Doo". To them that was a nickname and a mark of upliftment in their social status. On their notebooks, textbooks, household and living items they marked them with their current nicknames. Within their friends, they told them of their new nicknames. People whom they did not tell of such names equally heard of the latest development and therefore called and addressed them as such.

Notwithstanding the advices Nelson and Fabian received at

their homes to be of good behaviour, the boys still continued with their indecent ways of life. Things that were unacademic took most of their time instead of their primary assignment of studying. Both were absenting from classes very much. They were spending most of their time attending night clubs, dances, film shows among other things which are not academic in nature.

CHAPTER SEVEN

Afterwards, members of "Super Shark night club" in New Field town of Steadiers arranged a dancing competition for their members. Nelson and Fabian were members of the club. They registered for the competition with the stated amount of three Dinab per contestant. The club listed items to be won by competitors including a refrigerator, a television set and a table fan, as first, second and third prizes respectively among other consolation prizes. The organisers of the contest tagged it "the bigger ball".

Nelson and Fabian took victory at the contest as a challenge and as such worked seriously towards that. The boys rehearsed their dancing styles within and outside their school premises.

On the scheduled day, the boys attended the contest. They wore bougous, bleached and stone washed jean trousers and a T-shirt all to match; the fashion in place then. They also wore big white canvass shoes and a tartard face cap. One attire complemented the other, in ruggedness. The boys also drank some gin and smoked cigarettes. Their eyes turned red and they looked boyish and crazy in outlook.

Then came the contest. Nelson was the forth to dance. He danced to the admiration of many. His performance thrilled many spectators. Due to the applause Nelson received, he was allowed five more minutes to dance to entertain people the more.

After Nelson came Fabian to perform. Fabian danced so well to the admiration of many. People felt so happy at his performance that they also clapped heavily for him. However, it was not as much as they did for Nelson. Nelson's performance was as a result of the extent to which he prepared. Fabian too had prepared heavily for the competition and as such his pleasant performance was not a surprise. Other contestants performed too but non of them received the applause Nelson and Fabian received.

Before the result of the contest was announced, Nelson and Fabian were optimistic that they will emerge victorious. Even while the panel of judges were compiling the results, some people were already congratulating Nelson and Fabian. The boys received a lot of handshakes and applauses. When the head of the panel announced the result, Nelson came first while Fabian came second.

Fans and friends of Nelson and Fabian immediately carried the two boys shoulder high. In fact, the victor and his runner up were carried shoulder high for over ten minutes. Thereafter, Nelson and Fabian were given their prizes. The organisers of the competition also arranged a van that conveyed Nelson, Fabian and their prizes to where they wanted to go and drop their items.

Nelson and Fabian did not take their prizes to their school. They had suspected queries from the school authorities and took their prizes to their friend's house, a fellow student outside the school. After dropping their prizes at their friend's house, Nelson and Fabian returned to their school.

The following day, Nelson and Fabian rented a room near their friends house, furnished it with their prices; to use it as their guest house.

At school, some students who heard of Nelson's and Fabian's success at the dancing competition, who had all along been expecting the boys went to congratulate them when they saw them. It was all cheer and applauses when the boys came into their school. Their fellow students carried them shoulder high too. It must be noted that the two boys had obtained permission claiming that they were going home for the weekend when they engaged in the dancing contest. The school authorities therefore did not query or penalize the boys for leaving the school.

At their school the following day, the boys decided to change their nicknames from "Doos" to "Big Doos". They had thus upgraded themselves by attaching an additional word to their nicknames. Nelson took after the name "Big Doo Nel" while Fabian took after the name "Big Doo Fab". The young men made their new nicknames known to their fellow students who addressed them as such.

With their success at the dancing competition, the heads of the two boys seemed as if it wanted to touch the ceiling in their behaviour. They behaved as if they were a little bit crazy and naughty. They never took their studies seriously. They had the impression that their best was yet to come and that they were to win more successes in more social engagements.

One day, the Principal of their school luckily met Nelson's father at a marriage ceremony. The principal again informed Nelson's father orally of Nelson's poor attitude to his studies and style of life. Nelson's father felt so bad over the news. However, he did not expect the news as a surprise because of Nelson's poor first term examination result.

Nelson's father promised to come to the school the following day to see Nelson, caution and advise him to desist from all those misdeamanour enumerated by the principal about him. Before the Principal of the school and Nelson's father departed from each other, Nelson's father thanked Nelson's school Principal for alerting him of Nelson's bad behaviour at the school.

The following day, Nelson's father came to the school. Luckily he met Nelson at the school. But to his greatest surprise Nelson looked so serious with his studies. The Principal was not at the school that day. Nelson's father as a result could not believe what the principal told him about Nelson the previous day. Nelson's father however, advised Nelson to be of good behaviour at the school and to always take his studies seriously. Nelson who claimed to be of good behaviour all together promised to improve on his conduct. However, Nelson's father did not inform Nelson of what the Principal told him previously. Nelson's father only assumed that the Principal must be engaging in character assassination or was speaking from his past experience or was trying to talk against his son. Nelson's father went home with the assurance that his son whom he had known for a long time to be a good boy has not changed for bad and still a good student.

When the second term examination came, Nelson and Fabian performed poorly. They knew that they had performed poorly too and were optimistic of failing. When the boys met over their anticipated poor result, they deliberated on the matter and came out with something. They resolved to post their results to their parents at an address that will get to them and not to their parents. On the addresses written as that of their parents the boys put up Fabian's friend's address.

With that method, their results posted to their parents will get to Fabian's friend's post office letter box. Fabian's friend will therefore keep the letters for Fabian.

When Fabian and Nelson submitted the addresses of their parents/guardians whom their results are to be forwarded to, they wrote the names of their parents but used Fabian's friend's address as their parents' addresses.

The two boys were queried by the school authorities on why they had changed their parents address. That was right because their new parents address did not show conformity with what was obtainable at their individual file. The boys claimed that their parents have changed address and residential locations as a result of service transfer. The school authorities who had no time and chance for further enquiries believed what the boys claimed.

When the school vacated, Nelson and Fabian went home like others. As soon as Fabian got home, he alerted his friend on the letters he was expecting. Fabian informed his friend, Samuel who owed the letter box which they had used to receive their results to keep letters addressed to his father and to Mr. Johnson

Kenneth for him. Samuel promised to meet Fabian's request. Fabian did not tell Samuel of the content of the letters he was expecting.

When the results of the second term examination was released, Fabian's and Nelson's results were mailed to their parents with the addresses stated as those of the parents. Samuel received the letters in his letter box and kept them for Fabian. Samuel did not know what was contained in the letters and did not query Fabian on any thing at all or on the possible contents of the letters. Samuel simply collected the letters and gave them to Fabian.

During the holidays, Nelson's parents asked him of his results at least to know his performances at school. He told his parents that it could be that their results have not yet been completely compiled and that was why it has not arrived yet. Nelson had informed his parents that he did exceptionally well at the examinations and that he was optimistic of success. Nelson had shown some signs of seriousness on his academic work at home and his parents believed him in all that he claimed.

Fabian's story was the same. He told his parents that what had delayed their results could be that the school authorities had not finished with the compilation of the results. He said that those concerned with the compilation of the results were lazy and don't take their jobs seriously. He mentioned that the results could reach their house soon. Fabian however, stated that he did very well at the examinations and as a result his success was guaranteed. He expressed serious optimism on his success. Fabian's parents who had no time to verify the authenticity of Fabian's claims believed him. Fabian's parents were busy commercial people who had little or no time for non-commercial activities.

After the three weeks terminal holiday, the school reopened for the third and final term. Nelson and Fabian were brought to the school by their parents. The two boys were dropped at the statement of result. They just dropped the students at school and went back home.

Before both parents dropped their children at the school, they again advised them to be of good behaviour, to be hardworking, dedicated to studies and above all to be respectful to the school rules, regulations and authorities. They told their children the usefulness of education and the benefits one is bound to derive from it. On their part, the students promised to adhere to their parents' advices and instructions which they claimed were very useful and important. The boys knew that what was told them are useful. For Johnson Kenneth, he did not want to embarrass himself or anyone because of Nelson again.

When Nelson and Fabian met, they examined their actions and discussed on their results. Fabian brought out their results and showed them to Nelson. They discussed on the results and thanked one another for their plans which did not expose their waywardness. The boys laughed over the results and finally tore them into pieces. Each congratulated the other for a plan well executed.

It must be noted that the parents of both students gave their children a reasonable sum of money as their pocket money apart from their school and boarding fees for the third term. Nelson's parents who did not want Nelson to encounter financial difficulties at school gave Nelson a huge sum of money that will enable him take care of his basic needs at school. So also is Fabian's parent. Fabian's parents had equally given Fabian a reasonable sum of money to enable him live comfortably at school.

Nelson and Fabian as usual were living a life which the resources they had could not cope with or accommodate. They were living a life which by far outweighed the resources they had. They were using their money mainly in attending social engagements like clubs, dances among other non-academic activities.

After some time, the boys found themselves in financial crises once more. They had exhausted their money and had little or nothing left with them as pocket money while their tastes kept on rising. Later on, their money finished and the boys could not afford their basic needs talkless taking care of other needs. Expenses at the guest house the boys had outside their school facilitated the exhaustion of their pocket money.

Their rest house was highly furnished that any girl that visited the place found it difficult to leave the place. That also made the two students to spend most of their time at the guest house instead of staying at their school premises to study. They were buying foodstuff and cooking there too at the expense of their school food.

Later, the boys thought of how to raise money to continue with their bad style of living. At one of those discussions, the boys decided to be selling their books and using up their school fees. Both boys sanctioned the ideas and mapped out ways of executing that.

The boys sold off some of their textbooks to their fellow students. They also tampered with their school fees. At a time, they exhausted their school fees. Those acts by the boys helped them to raise some money which enabled them to cope with their adopted style of life. The "Big Doos' neither took chances nor compromised social life for anything else.

At one of the outside night parties which Nelson and Fabian attended, the boys drank heavily that they got intoxicated. The two young men never knew that they were drunk and intoxicated. Though they behaved abnormally on their way to their rest house. On their way, they ran into a Medical Practioner who was just walking to his house from his clinic after attending to an emergency call that early morning.

Nelson being so drunk abused the medical practitioner. Nelson asked the young medical practitioner what he was doing outside his home that early morning. The medical practitioner ignored Nelson whom he suspected was drunk. Nelson being rude went to the doctor, pushed him and asked him why he was feeling too big to answer his question. Nelson told the man thus "if you do not answer my question, I will kill you immediately". The medical practitioner was surprised on what he was seeing which he believed was an unexpected surprise. Replying, the doctor told Nelson thus "if you kill me will you be okay. I am returning from an emergency call and I am not in the mood to speak to anyone". Nelson did not accept what the medical practitioner was saying but instead gave the man two hot slaps. The man was highly offended that he was poised for action.

The medical practitioner replied Nelson with four hot slaps. The young medical practitioner was charged for more action, even awaiting for any likely action from Fabian who was trying to defend Nelson. Fabian on his side was not eager to fight for Nelson. He however tried to separate the two people who were already engaged in a physical combat.

Not happy with the development, the doctor was charged for more offence. He felt so unhappy over the development. He wondered why he should be abused in that way. He had considered himself innocent to be offended by anybody in that way. He further got hold of Nelson and gave him several hot slaps. During that severe heating, Nelson realised that he was drunk and intoxicated and was behaving abnormally. Nelson came to his senses then. Without wasting time he ran away with Fabian to their rest house. The medical practitioner wondered what was happening and concluded that the concerned men could be heavily drunk.

When the two young men got to their rest house, Nelson queried Fabian on what had happened. Fabian narrated to Nelson what happened. Nelson expressed disappointment over that. He told Fabian that he never knew when all those things that had taken place happened. Nelson thereafter told Fabian to be informing him when his actions go into excesses for his caution. He told Fabian that if actions get into excesses it could be disastrous. He had looked at his face and observed that he had been injured. Nelson and Fabian from that day learnt a bitter lesson.

Nelson really felt sorry over his acts. The boys made enquiries on the person they abused and found out whom he was and where he resides. Nelson decided to go to the doctor to apologize for his abuses to him. He left for the doctor's clinic with Fabian.

On getting to the doctor's clinic, the nurses at the place queried Nelson and Fabian on why they wanted to see their boss. The two young men narrated their experiences with the doctor that day's early morning and said that they had come to apologize to the doctor over what happened. The two students were given visitors' form to fill which was passed to the doctor later. The doctor later on, called in the two young men inside his office. Nelson and Fabian got inside the doctor's office and got seated.

Without wasting time, the two students informed the doctor whom they were. They further apologized to the doctor over what happened that day's morning between them and him. They regretted what happened and stated that they will never repeat such again. The boys mentioned that they were returning from a party that morning where they had got drunk.

Nelson however, mentioned that the type of beating and injuries he received as a result far outweighed the insult he rendered. He said that when a beating that is meant to correct a mistake outweighs the mistake then it does not worth the correction any longer. He said that such has thus become a punishment. He pleaded for his bad attitude but begged the doctor never to over react when provoked.

The doctor frowned at what happened. He said thus, "I was confused on the situation and was fighting on self defence. I apologize for any excesses on my part for I acted on provocation. I advise you to be dedicated to your studies. Take your academic work as your primary function before every other thing. One whose house is on fire needs not abandon the primary assignment of putting off the fire in pursuance of the rats that could be coming out of their hiding places of the burning house running for safety. Disregard all acts that could be detrimental to your studies and to your lives. We are responsible for creating our own reality and that man is responsible for his own creations. For one to succeed in life, the person has to accord his primary responsibility great attention more than other things. For one to be successful in life, the person has to first know what he or she want and then channel his or her efforts and energies towards achieving that goal. I am sure you learnt a lesson with your experience as one has to learn from experience and history. One who does not learn from experience and history is doomed for life. After harvest, all types of foodstuffs are kept at a place. Later, all are kept at their respective places. Yams are separated. Those that are to go to the barn are kept one side while those that are to be eaten as food are kept another side. Be of good behaviour, be honest, dedicated and take your education serious to justify the expense which your parents incur on your education. It is not the mistakes one makes that matters but what has been learnt from such mistakes. Never allow yourselves to be mixed with chaff when human beings are separated from one another. Keep off from bad companies who are bound to deceive you. One who is confident of himself needs not join others to attain his desired height. Be of good behaviour for your benefit, for the benefits of your parents and your generations, communities and your nation. The type of crop one plants determines the type of harvest the person gets. As a result, build a good reputation for yourselves and for your generations as a good legacy because the person that plants an iroko tree is not the person that makes use of it".

The man paused for a while and said "One day, you will come to live, stay, cater and manage yourselves. You will not live under your parents care all your life. There will be a time you will know that the world is not a bed of roses. A child being carried on the back does not know that the journey is of a long distance; thinks that the journey is sweet and unpaining and wants the destination to be extended". The doctor later on gave Nelson and Fabian one Dinab as a gift. The boys showed a high sense of remorse there and after thanked the doctor.

The doctor who was going to celebrate his seventh year of practice as a medical practitioner in two days time, invited the boys to come and celebrate with him. The doctor gave the venue of the celebration which he stated was his house. The boys promised to honour the invitation while promising to turn a new leaf of good behaviour. Nelson and Fabian thereafter left the clinic and the doctor.

With all the pieces of advises Nelson and Fabian received from the doctor, they changed their carefree attitude for the better. They started to shun all delinquencies and acts of indiscipline. Both had wondered how a person that is not in any way related to them had given them such advise. They considered the matter so serious and concluded that it should be accorded great attention. The boys had considered the advices very worthwhile. "If the advices had come from my parents I would have considered that as one of those statements in record albums that whenever they are put on music sets give exactly the same song", Fabian said. The young men therefore took their studies seriously, minimised their visits to their guest house, reduced the desire for ladies and were more in the school premises. There was a remarkable change and improvements in the lives of the boys after meeting with the doctor.

On the day of the doctor's celebration, Nelson and Fabian got set to attend the occasion. Nelson wore an outer short sleeve shirt that was smaller than the inner one. On their way to the celebration, the boys heard someone who shouted "England is bigger than Europe". The person shouted that and ran away while looking and pointing to Nelson.

As the boys went on for the party, Nelson who was confused on the statement made by someone who ran away saw someone and asked the person how England can be bigger than Europe. The person in his response told Nelson that what was meant by England is bigger than Europe was that Nelson was wearing an outer shirt that is smaller than the inner one which is supposed to be vise versa. Nelson changed his attire immediately and wore the smaller shirt inward and the bigger shirt outward.

At the doctor's party, all the guests were highly welcomed and entertained. During the toast, Fabian broke his glass cup which was filled with some wine, when he knocked his cup recklessly with that of Nelson. Fabian thought that toasting was hitting cups seriously. He never knew that it meant touching cups slightly by toasters. People's attention focused on Fabian for the abnormality. They looked at Fabian as a timid person. Fabian felt inferior before others at the ceremony and left immediately for school before Nelson and other people.

CHAPTER EIGHT

Nelson and Fabian had much in common. They were of similar character. When one became of good behaviour both changed for good at the same time. Throughout the period they were living a similar type of life both never quarreled. Ones opinion or suggestion was most of the time considered by the other without much argument. Both were like palm oil and salt that do not quarrel - are inseparable and has a lot of things in common.

As Nelson and Fabian changed for good, many people felt surprised over the development. Many teachers felt happy over the change. There was a time both wanted to sell-off their guest house. They discussed seriously on the matter but finally restrained action.

Nelson's form teacher who had expressed delight over the development had at Nelson's class said that "there is no body who does not have good things in him. Such good things can be developed with the appropriate machinery".

As time went on, Nelson and Fabian started changing for the bad again. Letters from girls they had met here and there were coming to them. Some kept informing the boys of their intending visits. Later on, parties and dances came into their lives again and the boys embarked on those their activities once more.

As the boys were into those activities, they did more than they were doing before. They considered themselves as having lost a lot of things during those periods they disassociated themselves from those engagements. They wanted to cover up all that they assumed they lost and therefore did all those things more than they were doing before. That time around, they spared no chances at engaging in rascality.

With the boys extravagant lifestyle and inordinate ways of behaviour the pocket money from their parents exhausted after a short while. It did not last long at all

When the pocket money of the boys got finished totally, they thought of a way of raising money to keep up with their adopted style of living. Later, they came up with an idea. They resolved to go to the seaport, harass aliens and extort money from them with the reason that they are not in possession of their required documents for their stay or that they have not paid their taxes, rates or one levy or the other. The boys resolved to carry out the operation from the following day at Tankoe seaport.

The boys agreed to be in their best attire preferably on suit with a tie to match in executing their operation. They resolved not to give room for lapses or suspicion that they are fake immigration officers or false tax agents, but to remain serious, stern,, courageous and outspoken. They chose not to entertain excuses, pleas or have any mercy on any illegal alien. They also agreed not to go after aliens that are many in number but to harass aliens that are alone. They stressed that whoever is healthy need not to take chances in the pursuit of money.

The following day, the boys went to the seaport to execute their plans. They were in their best attire of suit. They saw a lot of aliens in one activity or the other. The boys stayed at a place and monitored movement of people, aliens and sea workers. Some of those aliens that were used to the place and the seaport moved with a high state of seriousness. Those that were new to the place moved with uneasiness, fear and calm. Such people exercised great caution and carefulness in their movements, utterances and engagements.

The two students saw an alien that they observed was new to the country and possibly an illegal one. They resolved to harass the man with a view to extort money from him. When the boys got to the alien, Nelson asked him thus "where are your requisite visit or residential papers?" The man brought out his papers and showed to the boys. Then, Nelson said to him "Where is your tax receipts and seaport development levy?" The man said "I am a foreigner and have no reason to pay tax or levy".

But Nelson maintained that the government has stated that aliens should pay taxes and seaport development levies. After much deliberation on the issue, the alien gave the boys one Dinab to enable Nelson leave him alone. The boys maintained that the offence can only be exonerated by a three Dinab payment.

The alien gave the boys one more Dinab. The alien gave the money and left the place fast; almost running away. As the alien was going away the boys opened their teeth to the alien in amusement and laughed. They shook each other and congratulated   one another for a job well executed.

The two boys never knew exactly why the alien had left the place. They cannot tell whether he had left to contact the law enforcement agents to arrest them or for his safety. To avoid embarrassment, the boys changed location with the aim of avoiding trouble and also to operate elsewhere. They left for a destination far from the place they operated, almost a quarter of a kilometre from the place they operated before.

At their new place to execute their plans, the two young men stayed at a place and watched what was happening. They stayed at that place for a while before they pointed their next target. This time, an alien who was a quiet young looking man, lonely at a place sitting on a long stool, having some rest and watching at events going on. Nelson and Fabian fastly and boldly went to the alien. They brought out their student identity cards and showed it fast across the man claiming that they were tax collectors that check aliens taxes and levies and that their identity cards were tax collectors' identity cards.

The two young men stressed that they were government employees, who were responsible for tax collection and the checking of illegal aliens who evade taxes; when the alien tried to interrogate them. The alien who migrated into the country without the appropriate documents was griped with fear. He shivered so much and that made the boys think he has questions to answer. Without wasting time he offered Nelson and Fabian three Dinab as bribe to avoid trouble. The two boys persisted that the amount was too small to relieve him of all the offences.

The suspected illegal alien begged the boys to accept the money like that since according to him "one could temper justice with mercy". The alien said "I have been finding things difficult all through my life and have come into the country to see whether I can make both ends meet". The alien later gave the boys another one Dinab.

The boys claimed that they have heard of the alien as a dubious human being wanted by police for interrogation. They mentioned that it was as a result of their magnanimity that they considered taking from him such a meager amount for him to be set free. They said that if not because of the love they have for him they would have dealt with him decisively without any atom of mercy. The alien thanked the boys for their love and kind gesture and all parties immediately left that vicinity. The alien wondered how people who have not known him before can claim that they love him and that he was dubious.

Nelson and Fabian immediately changed from the place to another destination. At their new point of meeting, the two young men thanked one another for a job well done. They congratulated and embraced each other for a successful operation, and stated that their best was yet to come. Their new meeting place was about one hundred metres from that their second place of operation..

At their third place of meeting, the young men stayed at a quiet place and looked at events. They stayed there for a while looking out for an alien to extort money from. They stayed there for a while deliberating on the matter and finally looked out and observed an anticipated target. That was an alien who was carrying a briefcase and a big leather box on his left and right hands respectively and was making enquiries by asking someone a question. The young men quickly realised that the alien was a new one that has just come into the country.

The two boys fastly rushed to the alien, greeted him and stopped him. They quickly brought out their school identity cards from their pockets and showed same fastly across the face of the alien so that the man will not ascertain and authenticate the identity cards. They told the alien that they were officials of the tax office and were on revenue drive for the government which included taxes and ports development levy. The alien quickly offloaded his portfolio and bag and brought out his resident permit and other requisite documents that authorized him to stay in the country. He further showed the boys the papers contracting and engaging him with a service company in the country. The alien claimed that he has been waiting for a vehicle from the company he has come to work for to come and take him to the company's office but had not seen any. The alien even begged the two young men to assist him locate the company's correspondence office which he mentioned was within the seaport premises.

The boys refused but further kept giving reasons why the alien should give them money. The alien was surprised on what he was seeing and experiencing. He had expected assistance from the boys but instead had seen and experienced embarrassments.

Soon, just about five minutes of the arguments between the alien and the students, officers of the service company which the alien had come for and was expecting drove in with their official car. They were three in number in an official car. One person was the driver while two persons were the company officials. Immediately they saw the alien Mr. Nokel, the officers stopped. One of the officials of the company in the car opened the door of the car and came out. He embraced Mr. Nokel at once. Mr. Nokel who was annoyed then did not receive the embrace very well as a result of the embarrassments he had received from Nelson and Fabian. The other official also came out of the vehicle after some few seconds. Two of the officials were foreigners who knew Mr. Nokel.

As Nelson and Fabian saw the developments they started

escaping from the place of the incident. They did not want to run fast for fear of being suspected of one bad thing or the other. They quietly started escaping slowly.

The alien, Mr. Nokel told the officials that some people were embarrassing him; pointing at Nelson and Fabian, who were a little bit far from them then. He claimed that the concerned people wanted to extort money from him, possibly kill him and take away his belongings from him. The two officials ran after Nelson and Fabian to catch them. One of them got hold of Nelson. But immediately, Nelson and Fabian fastly gave that official some slaps on his face. The slap was in fact, severe that the concerned official became uneasy and shouted for help. The other official seeing the development ran back for his dear life, while Nelson and Fabian ran away as fast as they could for safety. They ran for sometimes and stopped in order not to be suspected of anything.

Thereafter, Nelson and Fabian walked fast heading to their guest house. They only stopped at a place, rested for a little while before they continued their clever walk which somehow was like running.

At their guest house, the boys thanked their Creator for safeguarding them from the problem they could have fallen into that day. In their prayers, the boys remembered God and thanked Him for his mercies. It must be noted that the boys have not been to church service for some time then. The matter made the boys to remember God.

That day, after their prayers, both counted their perceived blessings. They recounted the huge sums of money they had obtained by tricks. Nelson mentioned that "when one is not fast in life the person is meant to suffer." He stressed that "it is when sense supercedes sense that people say that tricks has been perpetuated." They congratulated themselves for a successful operation. They again enumerated their gains and mentioned the difficulties they encountered all through the processes. Both assumed that the material gains had far outweighed the problems experienced. Thereafter, the boys slept as they have not done before.

When the boys woke up, they were so pleased for having made so much money that will enable them carry on with most of their mapped out social engagements, which they considered of primary importance; which had lured them into deceitful acts. Thereafter, the boys changed their nicknames from "Big Doos" to "Hippies". To the boys the change of name was a mark of rise in their social status. Nelson picked up the nickname "Hippy Nel" while Fabian took up the nickname "Hippy Fab". After sometime, their new names circulated among their fans and friends who addressed them as such.

With the huge sum of money in the boys' coffers, their state of social engagements increased tremendously. It is believed that as one's income increases so also are the needs of that person; it increases also, all things being equal. It must be noted that the boys' attitudes and behaviour are all aimed at meeting their needs for social engagement mainly. With their huge sums of money, the boys head swelled as it never did before.

Two days after that seaport operation, information that some disgruntled human beings have been harassing and extorting money from people and aliens circulated mostly to the police and to the general public. The information was commented at the state radio and television station. At the news that alerted the public of the activities of such unscrupulous people, it was announced that people should be aware of the nefarious activities of some dubious people that harass innocent aliens at the seaport and extort money from them by pretences. The broadcast alerted the public to be aware of the activities of such individuals and report anybody engaged in such act or suspicious characters to the law enforcement agents or to the seaport officials. The information was announced several times at both the radio and television broadcast.

Nelson and Fabian heard the news on the television set in their guest house. They knew that their recent operation at the seaport must be instrumental to the announcements. When both boys heard of the news on their television set, they laughed over the news. They however concluded that they would not engage in that act within that period that the news had circulated and people and the law enforcement agents were all very much at alert.

They wanted to exercise some restraint at that period till tension on the news and the mapped out counter actions by authorities subside. That was proper since it is believed that "for whosoever the noisy moving train kills seems to be deaf". The boys however promised to strike again in future.

But with the extravagant lives the boys were living, all the money they had obtained from aliens by tricks still did not last long. They had doubled the number of girls they had as friends, bought more expensive shoes and clothings and doubled the number of clubs they belonged. They did not channel the money they had obtained by tricks into any meaningful venture, as it is believed that ill-gotten money is hardly put into meaningful use So, there was wastage on the side of the boys.

CHAPTER NINE

With the loot the boys cunningly obtained at the seaport, they at a time quarreled. The cause of that disagreement was on the use of their guest house. Fabian complained that Nelson was using their guest house more than him. He claimed that most of the time when he come to their guest house, Nelson was there with a girl. He therefore reiterated that Nelson was inconveniencing him. But the two understood why the situation was like that which is their relationship with girls. They therefore wanted to resolve the matter amicably.

They held a close door meeting in which they discussed on a way forward. At the meeting, both resolved that they should look for another guest house, furnish it to taste so that any of them could occupy it. They quickly looked around for another room and got one. The boys travelled home and got some money. They used virtually all the money with them to got their new guest house furnished. They bought almost all the living equipments that was in their first guest house and put it inside their new guest house. With all the money they had, furnishing their new guest house did not pose much problem to them.

After the furnishing of the new guest house came the problem of who will occupy it. Nelson and Fabian deliberated on the issue but could not find an answer to the matter. Later on, they used ballot system to decide on the matter. Nelson wrote on two pieces of papers the words "Yes" and "No". Nelson then folded the papers very well. He said that whoever pick up the one written "Yes" will take over the new guest house while the other person that picks up the other paper written "No" will stay at the old guest house. When the two folded papers were ready, Fabian was allowed to pick first. Fabian picked and collected the one marked "No", which indicates that Fabian was to stay at the old house. Nelson thereafter picked up the remaining paper which was marked "Yes". With that, Nelson is to stay at the new guest house. Both parties did not discuss on the house issue further since the scheduled plan to sort out the matter had been implemented and accepted by them. With that arrangement, Nelson went to occupy the new guest house while Fabian stayed back at the old guest house.

With both boys occupying different rooms, they increased their activities towards non-academic matters. Things that had little or no relationship to academics took most of their time. They were truants at school. They stayed at their respective guest rooms more than in their school.

There was a time that the school authorities noticed so much about the boys non-challant attitude to school and to academic matters. The school authorities wrote to the parents of both students informing them of the boys' attitude to classes. The letters got to the wrong addresses which Nelson and Fabian gave the school authorities as their current parents' addresses. The letter got to the owner of the letter box whom Fabian had informed earlier to keep letters to his parents and that of Mr. Johnson Kenneth for him. The letters to Mr. Johnson Kenneth and Fabian's father got to Fabian's friend's letter box and was kept safely for Fabian.

Nelson and Fabian received the letters addressed to their parents later. In the letters, their parents were advised to warn the boys on carefree attitude to studies, waywardness and against much engagements in non-academic activities. Nelson and Fabian read through the letters, laughed over it and tore same.

However, the school authorities had earlier queried Nelson and Fabian on why their parent addresses were the same. The two boys in their separate reply stated that their parents were working at one place and as such had one postal address. They claimed that they knew each other before they came into the

the school and that was why they had been friends and had maintained their relationship.

As the boys continued with their inordinate style of living, some money recently sent to them by their parents and the money they obtained by tricks from aliens at the seaport exhausted in wasteful exercise. The boys had increased their .desire for girls, increased their smoking habit, attendance to dances and clubs among other social engagements. The boys did not have a sound state of mind until the money exhausted. When the money finished, the boys then came to their senses. That was the time they started to live a normal peaceful life.

But as the desire for social activities was very much   boys, they tried to look for a way to raise money to meet their social needs. The boys had finished their money to the extent that they found it difficult to take care of their daily meals. With the rent they paid for their new guest house accommodation, another financial burden was further attached to them.

It must be noted that when one is in need of something the person goes for it. Since the resources the boys had could no longer take care of all their general needs, other ways of raising funds came into their mind.

The boys arranged to go to Cresland market to harass tax evaders and extort money from them. On the day they resolved to embark on the act, they scheduled to start off the following day. They did not want to give gap or take chances in that desire. They agreed to be in a good attire in order not to attract suspicion from anybody.

The following morning, the two boys went to Cresland market as planned. At the market, the boys were at a place watching market activities. They had resolved not to harass any person they deemed educated or well dressed who could ask them of their identity cards or could be a tax payer. Their target was the wretched non properly dressed people, whom they deemed could not differentiate their left from their right in terms of education and awareness.

The boys made a fortune on their first day. They harassed and extorted money from many people that first day. If the boys strike at a place, they will change base to another place all within that market. They did not take chances on whoever they deem was a prospecting target. After that first day of operation, they resolved to be going to the market to make fortune any day they consider themselves broke financially.

After that first successful outing, the boys still went to the market the following day. They abandoned their studies for the market with the aim of extorting money from some members of the public again. The boys had considered going to school that day but later took the option of going to .the market for operation. Fabian said that "business for money first before education". He stated that "education without money could be meaningless".

Anybody that the boys confronted for extortion brought out money. Even when the person had paid his tax, the boys must look for a loophole to perpetuate their evil act. For those one who brought out receipts of three years of payment of tax the boys would demand for five years of it. No matter the years of evidence of tax payment, the boys demanded for longer years of tax receipts. The boys looked for a way of extorting money from whoever they considered as their target in the form of bribe. They never took chances on any prospective target.

At most times, people who had paid their taxes just gave the boys money in order not to be embarrassed or delayed in their engagements. Some of those whom the boys confronted, were so much in a hurry that they did not want anything to waste their precious time.

That second day, the boys encountered a little problem during their operation. They saw a dumb man and requested from the man evidence of his tax payment. The boys talked to the dumb man for sometime but the man refused to say any word to them. Later on, Nelson tried to get hold of the man. The dumb man felt so offended and in retaliation picked up a big stone and threw at Nelson. The force of the stone thrown was so serious on the back of Nelson, Nelson suffered severe pain. Nelson felt perplexed and ran away for his safety. The boys and the dumb man ran away to different directions for safety. Nelson and Fabian met later on.

Nelson and Fabian forgot their bags at that spot as they were running away. Someone witnessing what happened at the place picked up the bags and ran away with it. The boys came back later at the spot they kept their bags but could not see them. With the lost bags, the fortune the boys made that day had been lost as the bags contained all the money they made. They did not want to continue with their operation that day after having that sad experience. The boys planned to abandon their operation that day and to reconvene the following day.

The following day, the boys came to the daily market as early as 8:00 a.m. in the morning. They did not want to take chances at all. They wanted to cover up what they think they lost the previous day and still make a lot of money. Because of that, they took their assignment that day more serious than before. Because the boys wanted to make fortune, they did not take into consideration those they had considered their target initially. They harassed and extorted money from any person they could lay hands on. They did that however, with some reservations putting into consideration little features of a deemed target.

But luck ran out for the boys that day. It is said that "everyday is for the thief but one day is for the owner of the house". The   boys saw a government officer who had come to the market to buy some things and harassed the man. The man looked a little bit casual and the boys had considered him a target. They went to the man and demanded his tax payment papers. The man frowned at the boys. The man works at the local council and knew those assigned to do tax/revenue service. The man also was an old serving officer at the local council that almost all the council workers knew him.

The man knew that the boys were not revenue officers and as such was highly offended at the boys dishonesty and impersonation. He therefore bounced on the boys. He first requested for the boys' identity cards as authorized local council revenue officers by saying "can I see your identity cards as genuine people, gentlemen".

The boys brought out their school identity cards and showed it across the man sharply. The man insisted that the boys should give him their identity cards for him to have a look at properly. The boys refused but rather persisted that the man should produce his tax payment papers or in alternative give them one Dinab.

The man felt aggrieved and immediately got hold of Fabian. At that time, the boys knew that the man must have seen them as impersonators. Fabian quickly pulled off the man's hands from him and both boys ran away with their bag. They did not miss their bag that day having had a bitter experience with their bag previously.

The man tried to pursue the boys but could not catch them. The boys ran for safety and met each other after a short while. They recalled their experience and thanked God for saving their lives from the consequences of impersonation which they could have faced.

The boys walked to Nelson's guest house. At the guest house, they upgraded themselves and nicknamed themselves "Big Hippies". Nelson took up the name of "Big Hippy Nelson" while Fabian took up the name "Big Hippy Fabian". But "Big Hippies" is for both of them.

In the night of that day, the boys watched their television set. At the news, it was reported that some people were impersonating as tax collectors and extorting money from the public. The information was signed by the Council Secretary. At the information that notified the public of the activities of such unscrupulous human beings, it was mentioned that people should first go through the identity cards of any person who claims to be a tax collector before showing the person any tax payment papers.

The information alerted the public to inform any suspicious character or any person claiming to be a tax collector when he is not, to the law enforcement agents or to the council authorities for arrest and interrogation. The information sensitized people to be at alert on that recent development.

Hearing all that on the television news, Nelson and Fabian knew that it was their encounter with the person that held them at the market that had prompted those statements. They laughed at the information. They concluded not to engage in that act meanwhile till tension on that subsides.

Soon afterwards, barely a month after the reopening of the third term, there came a raffle draw game organised by the Debating Club of Lawson Grammar School. With the line up of items to be won at the contest, the first prize was a big radio set, the second prize a table fan, the third prize an electric pressing iron among other consolation prizes.

Nelson and Fabian bought tickets for the contest. The boys even enrolled into the debating club and talked so good of the club. They thought that that will boost their winning chances at the contest. A ticket for the raffle was one Dinab. Nelson and Fabian bought four Dinab worth of the ticket each. They wanted to win at least one of the items slated at the contest.

From the day the boys enrolled for the contest, they kept praying to God to help them win. They knew that winning is what they should obtain by luck. The boys became sober, humane, disciplined and responsible, so that luck will be on their side.

On the day slated for the draw, a lot of people came to have a look at events at the place. Nelson and Fabian came earlier than scheduled. The time for the raffle was 12:00 Noon. Nelson and Fabian came around 11:30 A.M.

When the raffle was drawn, it was Joseph Kenn a young, mannered and responsible boy that won the first prize. The second and third prizes went to Samuel Doer and Maxwell Hunt respectively. They were all disciplined, reasonable and responsible boys.

None of the items among all the consolation prizes went to Fabian or Nelson. The boys were so much annoyed. Nelson reacting to the raffle draw result said to Fabian "I do not know why affluence most of the times go to those who do not know how to spend money and most of the time get hard for those who know how to spend it".

Later on, the boys' money finished. The boys decided to find a way to raise money and overcome their financial plights. The boys discussed on the matter and came out with a plan. They planned to go to the streets and extort money from beggars. The boys scheduled to execute their plan the following day.

The following day, the boys set off to implement their plans. The boys resolved that they would look as if they wanted to put money into the container in which a beggar uses to collect alms from people. But instead of putting money into the container they would rather collect money from the container.

As the boys set off to execute their plans, they kept praying to succeed. The boys kept succeeding. If the boys see a beggar they will sympathize with the beggar by gimmicks. They will rather pick money from a beggar's tray in the process of doing as if they want to put money inside it.

But luck ran out of the boys later on. There came a normal man who was pretending to be disabled and was begging. The man was in fact normal but was supporting himself with walking stick and looking tartared too. The man knew the amount in his alms tray.

When Fabian and Nelson saw the man, they sympathized with him over his condition and behaved as if they wanted to put some money on the man's tray. The boys rather collected money from the man's tray. The man who knew the amount that was on his tray discovered that it had reduced. He got offended and in turn removed his stick and raised an alarm over what happened.

The boys felt surprised immediately ran away for their safety. The man pursued the boys over a long distance till the boys got tired and posed for a fight with the man. The man seeing the development ran away. The boys ran away at once. As soon as the man saw that the boys were running away for the second time, he started pursuing them again. As soon as the boys saw that the man was chasing them stopped to get hold of him and beat him up. As soon as the man saw that the boys had been at a place to possibly catch him and harm him ran away. The boys laughed as the man claiming to be a beggar was running normally. The whole affair looked like a concert.

There, each congratulated the other for an operation well executed. The boys at once nicknamed themselves Jammers. To the boys, the name was an upgrade in their social status. Nelson took over the name "Jam Nel" while Fabian took over the name "Jam Fab". The boys counted the money from that operation and felt happy.

Two days later, the boys planned to go to the church to collect money. During their deliberation on how to make the money, the boys concluded to go to the offertory tray and collect money from the tray pretending to be putting money inside it.

The following day, the boys stepped-off to execute their plan. That day was a Sunday. In the church, the boys behaved and pretended to be good people as they sand and praised God with other worshippers. When people were called upon to make their church offering, the boys lined along with other worshippers. The boys went to the offertory tray several times and collected money instead of putting money into the tray.

The boys after the church service counted the huge sum of money they made from the deal. They thanked each other for the operation successfully executed. They laughed over the matter and in addition nicknamed themselves "Pullers". Nelson took after the name "Nel Pull" while Fabian took after the name "Fab Pull". To the boys that was an upliftment in their social status.

That singular boys' act reduced the range of money the congregation used to realise on offertory drastically that the church officials suspected foul play from members of the congregation.

The church officials who had suspected foul play took some

steps to remedy any possible anomaly that might have caused the reduced offertory. The officials decided to pass offering trays to members of the congregation to give their offertory instead of allowing people to come to the tray stand to put money during service time.

During the following church service, the officials implemented what they had resolved. During the offering, trays were passed to those at the church to put money and it was well supervised. Nelson and Fabian who had nothing to give, gave nothing. They assumed that their foul play the previous week has been detected. They smiled at each other while the tray was being passed to those in the church. After the church service, the boys laughed over the development and concluded not to go for church service for the meantime.

When Nelson and Fabian had their money finished again as a result of their inordinate lifestyle, the boys resolved to preach the gospel of God and sing christian songs to people in order to make money from them through donations.

The boys resolved to go to a far away place where they will not be known to the public as crooks to preach the gospel of God. A day after the conception of the idea, the boys set off to Satem, a known town to execute their plans. At the place, the boys went close to a primary school where people were gathered and started preaching the gospel of God and sang praises to God.

The boys sang very interesting Christian songs to those that gathered to listen to them. At intervals, the boys requested for donations from people. Many people there were happy to see young people turning to God and preaching Christianity. As such, many people donated generously. To make more money, the boys told those that were listening to them that the more they make donations, the more they will witness miracles and favours in their lives. As a result, many people donated generously and lavishly. Those that donated little were rebuked by the boys as being uncharitable and not real Christian hence does not deserve Gods Favours. The boys sang and sang; preached and preached to the admiration of many.

But luck ran out on the boys later that same day, when a teacher in their school drove along the place and saw the boys preaching. The boys sighted the teacher too and ran out of the place. The teacher came out, looked for the boys but could not see them. The boys met later at Nelson's guest house and there they counted the money they made from their outing. Both congratulated the other for a successful operation. There they changed their nicknames. Nelson took after the nickname "Yob Nel" while Fabian took after the nickname "Yob Fab".

CHAPTER TEN

Later, "Systems Night Club" scheduled a dancing competition which was tagged "The Bubble". The dancing competition was open to the public with a non refundable registration fee of one Dinab. Nelson and Fabian were members of Systems Night Club. They showed great interest in the competition. They had done such before and succeeded and entertained no fear as to their competence in winning.

Nelson and Fabian paid the non-refundable fee to enable them take part at the contest. The contest was to be held seven days from the date the boys registered. The contest was scheduled to take place on a Sunday.

Prizes for winners at the contest was also listed. The first prize was a refrigerator. The second prize a radio cassette tape recorder, the third prize a table fan, fourth price a wall mirror among other consolation prizes. Nelson and Fabian were confident of victory. They therefore had no fear of any failure in the forthcoming event. The boys prepared for the contest, rehearsing day after day leaving no stones unturned as it is believed that "God help those that help themselves". They rehearsed thoroughly their dancing styles. At their private rooms, the boys practised a variety of dancing methods. Each, at times, watched the other perform. That was to find out from each other the weak points and possibly point out areas of improvement.

The boys were not necessarily desperate for the prizes. They were more interested in boosting their status among their friends and fans and other rival champions.

Before the scheduled day of the dancing contest, Nelson

informed his close friend, Flomy among other girls named Bernadeth and Terry to go along with him for the contest. He individually told the girls to go with him. All the girls agreed to accompany Nelson to Systems Night Club for the contest. They were glad to be associated with a performer like Nelson. Each of them was happy for the privilege to be invited.

None of the girls ever knew that Nelson had invited another girl to accompany him to the contest talkless of girls. Each of the girls had the impression that Nelson invited only her and no other girl. Nelson on his part, had told the girls one after the other that he had not invited any other girl except her.

Nelson told the girls one after the other not to disappoint him since he had no other girl to go with and does not have the intention of taking any other girl to the contest. In fact, each of the girls had the impression that Nelson was taking her alone for the competition. They prepared heavily for the scheduled day with their finest attires.

On the part of Fabian, he invited two girls for the dancing show. Privately, he told the girls one after the other to accompany him to the contest. He had assured the girls individually that he did not invite any other girl. With the assurance the girls received, each was convinced that she was going to dominate Fabian at the occassion.

On the scheduled day of the competition, the invited girls came to Nelson and met each other. At Nelson's guest house, the invited girls quarreled among themselves that they even fought each other. It was a free for all fight among girls at Nelson's guest house. Flomy inflicted wounds to the other girls and finally left for the contest with Nelson.

At Fabian's guest house, the story was the same. The two girls came as invited and in the process of pushing out the other from the house each fought the other. Both wounded the other. The stronger girl who won at the fight went along with Fabian for the contest.

At the contest, there was about twenty contestants. News of

Nelson's and Fabian's enrolment had circulated very much among the other contestants. Many people have heard of the boys' excellent performance sometime ago in dancing contest. Many people were around expecting the boys. With what was heard of the boys with regards to dancing, some people considered the boys success at the competition a sure victory.

Nelson and Fabian were the ninth and tenth performers at the show. They enrolled at the same time and as such their numbers were consecutive to each other.

Those who were to dance before Nelson and Fabian performed. They were hurried by enthusiastic spectators to finish up to enable Nelson and Fabian perform. Thereafter, Nelson and Fabian took their turns. Nelson and Fabian were each carried shoulder high when each was called upon to perform. The boys danced very well to the admiration of many. The boys had prepared well for the show and no wonder they did the much expected magic. The boys danced and changed their styles of dancing as the music for their dance changed.

Due to the admiration people had for the boys' performance, the boys were allowed to perform for fifteen minutes each while other contestants were allowed only ten minutes each. After the boys (Nelson and Fabian) had danced, the other contestants after them performed too. But none of the other contestants received the type of applause Nelson and Fabian received.

As the results for the contest was being compiled, many people presumed that Nelson and Fabian will excel at the contest. Some people were already congratulating them. People knew that the boys had performed creditably well and as such were meant to come out victorious if all things remain equal and if no signs of manipulation or favouritism exist.

When the panel of judges for the competition announced the results of the contest, Nelson came first while Fabian came second. Nelson and Fabian were at once carried shoulder high by their fans and well wishers. They were later on presented with their prizes. Thereafter, other winners were presented with their prizes and the contest ended.

With that brilliant success, Nelson and Fabian added another feather to their cap. Their victory spread everywhere like harmattan fire within and outside their school premises.

Each of the boys went home after the contest with his lady and prize. At Nelson's guest house, the boys changed their nicknames to "Stormers". That was to them an upliftment in their class and status. Nelson took up the nickname "Nel storm" while Fabian took up the nickname "Fab storm". But stormerswas their general name.

With the boys' success at that dancing contest, Nelson and Fabian became more carefree to studies. They behaved as if they were in a class of human beings far more than what could be obtainable for an ordinary student. They behaved in a more saucy and naughty manner. Since the boys' lifestyle was such that their resources could not cope with, the boys soon afterwards exhausted all the financial resources they had. However, the boys never got bothered, since they were satisfied with each other, even though their happiness is artificial.

After about seven days of their dancing outing at Systems Night Club came another dancing competition at Style Club. That was also a big dancing contest tagged "Big jump". The boys registered for the contest with the non refundable fee of one Dinab. The boys knew that they were up to any dancing task and therefore did not entertain any fear while registering for the contest. Normally, one hardly venture into any engagement in which the person is not sure of any meaningful result. The boys knew that they were equal to any dancing contest and therefore registered.

Before the date of the contest, the boys had contacted their girls to accompany them to the contest. The girls agreed. The girls were the ones the boys invited at their last outing. But the girls had entertained fear that they could encounter what they experienced the last time. They therefore did not honour the invitation on the scheduled date even though all of them agreed to come.

Unfortunately, on the scheduled date of the contest, none of the girls came to accompany either Nelson or Fabian to the contest as the boys waited. After waiting for so long without seeing any girl, Nelson came to Fabian's guest house and both departed for the contest from Fabian's guest house. The two boys went without any girl accompanying them. It was a sad experience for the two boys.

At the contest, there were only eight contestants. The reason for the low number of contestants was that intending contestants were scared of Nelson's and Fabian's enrolment.The dancing expertise of the boys had been known and acknowledged by so many people who deemed it a waste of time competing with them. Some people who even came to the contest were there to have a look at Nelson and Fabian; nothing more. Some people who enrolled for the contest only wanted to try their luck since it is believed that "there is no harm in trial".

At the contest, Nelson and Fabian had the forth and fifth performance respectively. They performed to the admiration of many people at the dancing hall. The result was later announced and Nelson and Fabian had the first and second position respectively. Even before the results were announced, people had anticipated victory for Nelson and Fabian. It was not a surprise to many of those at the hall who had been carrying Nelson and Fabian shoulder high. The boys were thereafter given their prizes along with the other winners.

CHAPTER ELEVEN

When the boys set to leave the contest hall, they were deeply drunk and almost misbehaving. Nelson later saw a girl whom he admired at the hall. He called on the girl and the girl came to answer the dancing champion. Nelson introduced himself to the girl. The girl later introduced herself to Nelson. Nelson excused the girl outside the hall. Fabian thereafter followed Nelson and the girl. The boys were tensed up for a love making affair.

Outside the dancing hall, Nelson requested for a love making affair from the girl. The girl claimed that she was knowing Nelson for he first time that early morning and therefore regarded the love making issue too early and unimportant. The girl named Christy bluntly refused the love making request from Nelson. Nelson being desperate to have the affair with the girl at that time tried to force her. He was assisted by Fabian and both raped the girl. The boys held Christy tightly by force to enable them force themselves unto the girl. The girl kept crying for help and later many people ran to her rescue.

Some people who saw what happened were disappointed. They expressed surprise on how Nelson and Fabian the acclaimed and renowned dancing champions could behave that way. There was confusion all over the place that the Police was contacted immediately. The third runner up at the contest who was annoyed with the boys triumph quickly alerted the police.

TThere were two policemen who were at the club to maintain peace and order. The two policemen arrested Nelson and Fabian. Before Nelson and Fabian were whisked off from the place, they were given serious caning by the policemen. The boys were immediately taken to Newtown Police Station and detained. That was the first time the two boys were having problem with the police and were also entering the police station.

When Nelson and Fabian came to the police station, those who were already in the police cell shouted for joy. Many of them clapped their hands while some sang songs of praises to God. They were all expressing their happiness on the forthcoming inmates. Most of the cell inmates asked the boys whether they had brought some gifts and items for them or not. Those inmates were speaking through a small opening in the cell. Some said that they would deal ruthlessly with the boys if the boys did not bring meaningful gifts to them. Some inmates said that if the boys had not committed any serious offence before being sent into the cell, the boys should see themselves in serious trouble and would be dealth with mercilessly. Most of the cell inmates were seen saying series of things all to welcome the intending inmates. Nelson and Fabian were seen confused at the development.

Some of the things which some of the cell inmates asked the boys were "what did you bring for me? What of my cigarette, I hope you came with it? I hope you brought some money to me? The gate fee is ten Dinab, I hope you came with it? My entrance fee is one Dinab, I hope you came with it?". These and more were what the cell inmates said.

With all the above comments the boys wondered whether the cell inmates had given them anything to keep for them or if they were owing those skeletal looking cell inmates. Later on, the boys' particulars were documented by the policemen on duty.

As soon as the boys were pushed into the police cell some of the inmates already in the cell got hold of the boys, and gave them a merciless beating. The boys were beaten up with severe anger that they cried out aloud for any possible help from anywhere, which never came. In fact, the boys have never received before that type of beating they received that day at the police cell. After the beating, Nelson said to Fabian "some people are satan here on earth".

Later on, the boys were called up by the other detainees for questioning. The boys were under the examination and interrogation of a panel of cell inmate judges under their distinguished Chairman. The Chairman asked the boys what they had done to be sent to the police cell. The boys were told to say the truth as fallacy must be viewed with a high level of seriousness. They were asked to be fast in their narrations.

Explaining what had happened to them, Nelson told the panel thus "we rape a girl and that was why we were taken to the police cell". The Chairman of the panel responding said "the offence was such a minor one". He ordered that Nelson and Fabian be given another serious beating by the entire inmates. The boys were again given another terrible beating by those hardened crime minded inmates.

After, the inmates bounced once more on the boy seven without being ordered to do so. Observing that the situation had become tough and unbearable, Nelson immediately brought out the only one Dinab in his pocket while Fabian brought out the two Dinab remaining with him. The two boys gave the money to those inmates. The inmates searched the boys thoroughly and found nothing more with them.

Nelson and Fabian cried and called on the police to come to their assistance and rescue them. The police heard them but pretended as if they were not hearing the boys. The police knew that such practice was normal inside that police cell and therefore did not want to interfere with what is obtainable in the cell. That was what was referred in that cell as "sanctification".

The police used the boys particulars to reach the boys parents, Principal and Form Masters. That same day, all those reached came to the police station to check Nelson and Fabian. Before they could come to see the boys, the boys had gotten slim that their eyes were almost inside their head. That was as a result of the severe beating and embarrassments they had suffered from the other cell inmates.

Nelson and Fabian's parents, Form Master and Principal saw

one another at the police station. To the parents of the students, it was confusion all over. They could not believe what they saw. They wished that day never existed. But to the Principal and Form Masters, they had expected that development because they had noted that the concerned boys were carefree, wayward, non-challant to studies and unrespectful. The police narrated to the parents, Form Masters and Principal of the concerned students what the students did and what it had earned them which is detention at the police cell.

The Principal of Lawson Grammar School, Mr. Samuel Dowin, told the parents of the concerned students their children's bad attitudes at school which led to the failure of the students at their first and second term examinations. He mentioned that the students were truants, carefree and undedicated to studies. He mentioned that he had personally to them on their children's activities and behaviour at school.

The parents of the students asked whether the results of the second term of the students had been released. The Principal said that the results had been released long ago and had been posted to the parents and guardians of all their students. He said it was done during the second term holidays. The parents of the students felt surprised on what the Principal said. They could not believe what they were seeing, hearing and experiencing. Their children had told them that their second term results had not been released.

CHAPTER TWELVE

elson's father asked Mr. Samuel Dowin if Nelson ever broke something called amoeba at their school laboratory. Mr. Samuel Dowin replying said there was never a time Nelson broke any equipment at our school laboratory or anywhere. Nelson does not normally come to school what more coming to the laboratory and breaking a laboratory equipment. Amoeba is not even an equipment but a micro-organism that cannot be seen by the naked eyes what more being broken by a human being".

Further, Mr. Johnson Kenneth went to the form master of Nelson's class and asked him if there was a time their class requested from their students books apart from that written on the prospectus. The form teacher in his response said "there was never a time my class requested students to buy books other than those listed on their prospectus".

The parents of the boys stressed to the form teachers of the students and the Principal that they had not received their wards second term examination results. They mentioned that their wards once came to them with non-existent books and obtained some money from them through pretence claiming that they would buy the books at school. They said further that what had just happened was "an eye opener" meant to expose what has been happening on the part of their wards.

The Principal asked Mr. Johnson Kenneth whether he had changed address apart from the address he used to have before. Mr. Johnson Kenneth said that he had not changed any address for the past ten years. The same question went to Thompson Daniel, Fabian's father. Mr. Thompson Daniel said that his address had remained what it used to be for the past six years

The Principal commented that "why Mr. Kenneth and Mr. Daniel have not received their ward's results about their behavior could probably be because of the wrong addresses given by their children. The boys knew they would fail their second term examinations and as such did not want to let their parents know of their failure and as such gave wrong addresses as that of their parents so that their parents would not receive their results. Normally, at every examination, one accesses himself or herself personally to know whether he or she will pass the examinations or not. The boys had accessed themselves after their examinations and had found out that they were not making any headway towards success and as such had given a wrong address as their parent's address".

The Principal, Form teachers and parents of the students were all talking in front of the police cell. Nelson and Fabian were inside the cell blinking their eyes and listening attentively to all those discussions. At that time, they had felt really sorry for what they had done and for what they had failed to do.

However, it is said that "whoever is to be killed must be allowed to make defensive statements". Nelson looking out through an opening from the big strong wall of the cell said some words to the hearing of his parents, principal and form teacher. He told his principal thus "for you to have said the bad in me without first saying the bad in you seems as if you are as white as snow. My principal is a bad man who has never taken his job seriously. If my principal is a good person his students should not have been found in such a situation. My principal has failed to do his duties, failed to do what he ought to do and as such had seen things in disarray". The Principal, commenting, said "Nelson and Fabian are not fair to me. I did my best to assist the boys morally". The following day, the boys were charged to court for rape and assault. The parents' of the students, their principal, form masters and a defence counsel were at the court to witness the the trial of the students. When the case came up for hearing, the Prosecuting Police Officer (PPO) told the trial woman magistrate that "Nelson and Fabian were caught the previous day raping an innocent girl thereby assaulting her". The boys also made oral and written statements. The concerned girl make statement and narrated what happened and how it all happened. But the boys pleaded not guilty to the charges while their defence counsel made submission and pleaded for mercy for the accused. Two people who witnessed what happened testified against the boys.

The trial magistrate frowned at that development. She said "I blame parents and school authorities for the growing state of juvenile delinquencies in our society. This is as a result of poor family upbringing and training. Most parents find it hard to devote their time towards the education and proper upbringing of their children but rather devote more time in money making activities while the morals of their children suffer. Such is risky to the nation and if unchecked, could lead to doom for the nation. On the part of children, those that choose to engage in rude activities are bound to suffer in various ways. Sufferings could be in the form of imprisonment to public assault. I plead with parents and school authorities to look into the activities of their wards for the good of the nation and for themselves. I have found the boys guilty of rape and assault. Justice must be done no matter whose 'ox is gored'. These boys will be imprisoned for one year each without any option of fine". After the judgment, the boys cried aloud for help which did not come from anywhere.

After the judgment, the parents of the boys felt so unhappy but realised that they could not do much to help as at that time. They felt bitter and cried.

Commenting after the judgement, The Principal Mr. Dowin said "I know that such a period will come to these boys. The boys have been in bad manners for a long time. The boys have just paid for what they asked for. 'Any mouse that comes out so often to where people always stay must be killed one day; it is just a question of time'. These boys have never looked smart, agile and interesting before their fellow students and the school authorities because they had a lot of useless activities to think about. A sound mind brings a sound idea, a sound body and sound life. All those things that are deceitful and unacademic will always be the portion of unserious students unlike things that are meaningful, reasonable and responsible. What one has weighs the   person nothing more".

The Principal and form teachers thereafter left the court premises for their school. They were followed by Nelson's and Fabian's parents who headed to their respective homes after giving their wards one Dinab each respectively to enable the boys take care of themselves in prison. Nelson and Fabian were later whisked off by the law enforcement agents and put inside the police van already waiting. They were driven to the main prison handcuffed. The documents that sentenced them to jail had also been taken along with the boys. The papers and the boys were handed over to the prison authorities accordingly and signed for. When the boys were brought to the prison reception, prison inmates who saw them rejoiced. Some sang songs of praises to God. They knew that new inmates had come to meet them. Many prison inmates danced and jubilated. Some from many corners asked Nelson and Fabian whether they had brought a reasonable thing for them or not. Some inmates told the boys that they would deal ruthlessly with them if they had nothing for them. Nelson and Fabian were all along confused over the situation they had found themselves.

From varying corners shouts of "I hope you came with my one Dinab? I hope you have my Indian hemp (wewe) with you? You will give me whisky. What of my gin? I hope you came with my cigarettes. I hope you came with my brandy? among other queries. It should be noted that some of the prison inmates have not tasted brandy or whisky before. Also, some of the prison inmates addressed hemp as we-we.

Later, Nelson and Fabian had their handcuff relieved from them by the policemen that brought them to the prison. The policemen thereafter left for their station.

As soon as Nelson and Fabian were taken into the prison by prison warders, the hungry, angry and tartardly dressed prison inmates pounced on the boys and had them beaten up mercilessly. The boys shouted and cried for help which did not come from anywhere. Beatings rained on the boys heavily to the extent that stars came out of their eyes.

As the prison inmates were beating Nelson and Fabian money felled out of the pocket of one of the prison inmates beating Fabian. Nelson picked up the money with the intention of returning it back to the owner.

The prisoners who were there under their distinguished Chairman later on (after the boys beating) called upon the boys for interrogation. There, a panel to interrogate, the boys was constituted under their Chairman.

The boys were matched out and were asked to stay at the centre before the panel members. The Chief Whip among the panel members asked the boys to cross their hands over their back and sit on the floor before other things. The boys who were afraid and confused did as were directed.

The Chairman of the panel sat on a sit to address Nelson and Fabian. He said "This is a full-fledged republic where all the various arms of government is fully in place - the legislature, the executives and the judiciary. Some governments may not have all these arms of the government. However, all the various arms are under my control. My decision in this republic is final. No one questions my judgement at all. If I say that someone should die in this republic that person is killed outright. If I say that Mr. A should live Mr. A is given life to live. No one questions my authority as far as our republic is concerned. Newland Republic is absolutely uninhabitable but you have to adjust your lives to live in it for there areno two ways about it. I have the right to do anything as far as our republic is concerned. I am the god of this republic. I have the right to kill, to allow one to live, to make one feel happy and so on. It is only to release a prisoner that I cannot do but I can make recommendations to the authorities concerned on such a matter. With my recommendations such could be possible. My name is Professor Lawlessness otherwise called Mr. Samuel Newmal. I am a Chief Judge of Law. I am the alpha and omega, the all in all in law, the omnipotent, omniscient and omnipresent of law. I hold M.Sc. in Law and Engineering."

The Vice Chairman of the panel said "I am Doctor Treatment, otherwise called Mr. Nathan Dowel. I am a doctor of prisoners. I have a B.A. Honours in medicine and appendix doctor".

The Secretary said "I am a professor of women. I can impregnate forty women a day and will neither get satisfied nor get tired. I love sex for it really touches my brain. To me, sex is the sweetest thing on earth; sweeter than honey. Nothing can be compared to it. Absolutely nothing. I have been to many places but I am yet to see something as interesting as sex. It makes me feel real happy. I have been to the east, west, north and south but I am yet to see something to rival sex. Sex in the form of rape took me to the prison; and I have no regret for my action. I feel on top of the world whenever I am having sex.I can die for sex. I can also live for sex. I am a sex addict. Sex can move me more than money. Women who cannot be impregnated can contact me for the right services; free of charge. Some people call me woman taster".

He smoked his hemp for a long time before he turned to Nelson and Fabian. He asked Fabian, "do you have a sister?" Replying Fabian said "yes sir". Again he said to Fabian "can you bring your sister to me for a test case. Some people can regard me as a foolish man for claiming to be a professor of women instead of being a professor in other things, it does not matter for everyone has his destiny and life to live. But I pray I will one day be rescued and be rehabilitated". At that point Fabian and Nelson laughed. The man gave Nelson and Fabian a hot slap each using his left hand for Fabian and his right hand for Nelson.

Continuing the Secretary said "I am a kind man who gives services to women free of charge. I can give women twenty four hour sex service a day so far they are pretty. In terms of women, I am an expert; a professional".

Looking at Fabian and Nelson, the Secretary shouted "do you chase women?" Nelson and Fabian in their response shouted "no sir, no sir" believing that such could portray them as good people to receive sympathy. The secretary felt aggrieved over the boys' reply and gave each of them a slap again. He said "men that neither chase women nor smoke are often wicked, unaccommodating, meticulous, foolish and selfish".

At that juncture, Nelson and Fabian felt highly offended and posed for a revenge. But rains of beatings came from the hungry, angry, malnourished and skeletally looking prisoners and that stopped them. The boys cried and cried aloud and stayed calm thereafter.

One other slim and tartard looking prisoner said "my name is Mr. Jobber; a specialist in sexually transmitted diseases. I love sex too much and that is why I specialized in sexually transmitted diseases.I am notorious with sex and that is why some people call me breast master while others call me mister skirt and blouse. I have B.A. in Disease Control. I also have a B.A. in eye doctor. I also trained in judgment. I have a B.A. in Justice Engineer".

The Assistant Secretary said "I am Doctor Henry Johnson. I am a Barrister of Mathematics". The Publicity Secretary said "I am Engineer Hardman. I am an English Language Engineer. I have moulded heavens here on earth. The Chief Whip shouted "I have a B.A., SPC, PCM, AYZ, TCM, PYY& AYZ in Building Technology. I also have M. A. in Computer Arts. I am the omnipotent, omniscient and omnipresent in building things. Other officers addressed themselves each attaching big titles to the real name. They were not reasonably educated either. In fact, they did not know what they said and claimed.

The Chairman of the panel who also claimed to be the Commander-in-Chief addressing Nelson and Fabian and pointing at Nelson said "you should be reporting on a daily to me or to my Vice if I am not available". He pointed to Fabian and said "you should be reporting to my Vice". Again, he said to the boys "you should serve us as you would like to be served. Nothing can be compromised for that at all. If you boys refuse my instructions you should consider yourselves dead. Our republic operates a paramilitary if not a purely military government in which everyone obeys to the last order" Nelson and Fabian promised to serve their appointed masters with all their heart, interest and zeal.

The Chairman of the panel then asked the boys the offence they committed that made them to be sentenced to jail. The boys almost at the same time said "we raped a girl". Before the boys could finish their reply, the prisoners pounced on the them and got them beaten up again.

After the beating, the Chairman of the panel said, "I frown at your reason for being sent to prison. While others commit atrocities like assassination, armed robbery, arson among other inhuman activities to earn reasonable jail term, you committed this minor offence". The Chairman of the panel ordered other prisoners to beat up the boys again. Some of the prisoners bounced on the boys and had them beaten up as directed. The boys cried. Tears rolled down their cheeks. Blood flew from their nose.

Later, the Chairman of the panel gave the boys a hot slap each, using his left hand for Nelson and right hand for Fabian. The Chairman said that the slap was from a head who is meant to have the last but greatest of anything being shared. The Chairman also used a pin to scratch the penis of the boys. The boys cried the more. The Chairman of the panel said to Nelson and Fabian "what did you bring for us?" Nelson in his response said, "I have brought nothing for you. I did not expect to come to the prison for anything and as such made no provisions for prisoners". When the prisoners heard that nothing was brought for them, they pounced on the boys once more and had them beaten up once again.

Nelson and Fabian seeing the chaotic situation brought out all the money they came into the prison with which was in their pocket. None of the boys actually knew when money was brought out. When the prisoners saw the money, they restrained further actions on the boys. Nelson and Fabian at that time were almost worn out, tired, confused and could not believe what they were seeing.

The Chairman of the panel asked Nelson and Fabian to introduce themselves. Nelson introducing himself said "I am Professor Nelson; a professor of fun. I am the biggest fun creator in the universe". Fabian said "I am Doctor Fabian; a doctor of love. I am the biggest love maker in the whole world. I hold a PTY, TCPC, MCM, DPT, TCY, B.A and TYPM in love making". The prisoners shouted "professor, doctor, professor,doctor, prof, doc and so on, hailing, shaking hands and clapping for the boys. They further carried the boys shoulder high to show solidarity.

The Chairman of the panel collected Nelson's and Fabian's money and handed over to their treasurer for custody.

Addressing Nelson and Fabian at that juncture, the Chairman of the panel said to the boys, "you are welcome. You have been initiated into our republic. Every human being that comes to this republic must be initiated into our fold just like any other person, irrespective of the person's social status or educational background; no partiality. An Ex-Governor who embezzled his state's money was initiated just like every other inmate. Some people did not believe that but it happened. I personally dished out the baptismal slap here in this republic. Feel at home. Report to other inmates or to the prison authorities whenever you are in difficulty. Members of the executive, legislature and judiciary are always at your service. Come out when all other prison inmates are asked to come out and participate in whatever other prison inmates are doing. The decision of my executive is final and binding on all inmates as far as this republic is concerned. That is my message".

At that juncture, Nelson handed over the money he picked to

its rightful owner. Nelson said to the Chairman of the panel, "I picked some money that felled from the pocket of a prisoner and have given it back to the rightful owner". Nelson thought he would receive commendation for his action. But in his response, the Chairman frowned and said to Nelson, "You can never be a wealthy man on earth. You are a big fool. Do you know what some wealthy people do to make money? People steal, kill, cheat and commit all sorts of atrocities to make money but you saw money at your footsteps and picked it and gave it to the owner. You will in fact, remain poor on earth". He ordered other prison inmates to get hold of Nelson and beat him up. Many prison inmates got hold of Nelson and got him beaten up.

It must be noted that the act of bullying a new prisoner or prisoners by other prison inmates to welcome a prisoner or prisoners into Shotaran Prison was known as "initiation" or "fire baptism".

After a while, other prisoners left the initiation ground leaving behind Nelson and Fabian. Nelson and Fabian went to one corner to have some rest. Later on, two prison warders brought to the boys their prison attire. It was at that time that the boys knew that they were prisoners. The boys remembered their descent homes they left to come into the prison to suffer. They remembered all the good things they used to enjoy before. The boys wept over the unfortunate incidence that made them to be imprisoned.

The prison warders laughed as they were with the boys. They however pretended as if they never knew what must have happened to the boys. They had spent some time before coming to see the boys to allow a reasonable time for the boys' initiation; for they knew what was obtainable at that prison.

However, Nelson and Fabian complained to the prison warders of other prison inmates harsh treatment unto them. The prison warders expressed concern over the whole affair and promised to look into the matter and possibly deal ruthlessly with other prisoners if they actually offended them. The boys signed for and collected their prison dresses. The boy felt aggrieved as they signed that. The prison warders asked the boys to put on their prison dresses immediately. The boys acting like obedient servants who act at the slightest instruction of his master put on the prison dress at once. The prison warders showed the boys one of the caravan rooms for their stay.

The room had two spring iron beds and two grass mattresses. The grass mattresses were so old and had series of distracting tiny insects inside them. The boys seeing their new place of inhabitance felt unhappy. They had compared the place with their guest house, their good beds at their homes and at their dormitories. Looking at the place, Nelson told one of the prison warders thus "this place is uninhabitable". The prison warders laughed at Nelson's statement and ignored him.

The prison warders further told Nelson and Fabian to always go for their food whenever the bell for that is rang. They promised to be visiting the boys from time to time to take care of their welfare. They also told the boys that they will bring an insecticide to kill off the insects later. They left. That same day before night came, one of those prison warders came with an insecticide. He sprayed the insecticide at the boys' room to kill insects and dropped it for the boys to be using from time to time.

CHAPTER THIRTEEN

When it was dinner time for the prison inmates, the bell for that was rang. All the prisoners rushed out to their refectory. Food was served. The quality and quantity of food served to the prisoners was poor compared to what should be given to a normal human being. The food served for dinner that day was a fairly cooked beans. Nelson and Fabian complained to themselves of the poor quality of the food they were served. They laid the complaint to the Chairman of the republic and to those serving the food. All the people that received the report laughed at the- boys. They knew that such was the type of food obtainable at the refectory and therefore ignored the complaint.

That night, Nelson and Fabian had severe stomach trouble. That worsened their already deteriorating health. However, the boys found out that they had little to do to change the already existing situation of things at the new place they found themselves. The boys compared the standard of living of their homes and guest houses with that obtainable in the prison and had found a great difference between the two. Nelson had during a conversation with Fabian said "It is the harsh treatment that prison inmates receive while in prison that make them terrible, wicked and arrogant at the prison". However, the boys resolved to adjust to the new place despite odds.

The following morning, Nelson and Fabian gave their republic masters the best of services they could afford. They went to the water tap and fetched water for their masters. They also washed their masters' clothes including their dirty pants. There was no soap at the place, so the boys washed the items without soap. They cleaned their dirty rooms too. The boys wondered how people could be living in such a state of misery and untold hardship.

The time of breakfast came. The bell for that was rang and prison inmates rushed to their refectory for food. The skeletal looking inmates were seen hurrying and running from various areas to the refectory. Most of them were running so fast in a manner that people least expected of them. Nelson and Fabian who were new to the system and are not used to that were seen going to the refectory gently. On their way, Nelson's master saw him and asked him and Fabian to hurry to the refectory like others. He told the boys to discard the idea of gentility in their republic. He said "there is neither gentility nor a gentlemen in our republic as we run almost a military state".

At that day's afternoon, Nelson's and Fabian's parents came to visit the boys at the prison. The first to come was Nelson's parents. Perceiving the sight of his son Mrs. Catherine Johnson Kenneth (Nelson's mother) wept at the prison reception where Nelson was called out for his parents. Lamenting, Nelson's mother expressed dissatisfaction at the state she saw her son. She said "this place is not the ideal place for my son I love and cherish so much and whom I bore in my belle. Whatever had led my son into such a place was a regrettable exercise which could have been avoided. I hate nonsense because nonsense does not help anyone. In life, one should ask himself what one has done to productivity, creativity, humanity and education and not what one has done on nonsense which does not take one anywhere".

While with his parents, Nelson said to them "you did not give me good moral training and that is why I have derailed and in prison today". Responding his mother said "it is your carelessness and stupidity that has brought you here". Nelson's father, Mr. Johnson Kenneth said to Nelson "the penalty that people pay for disobedience could be severe as it is the case with you. If lessons are not taught to one, the person can hardly learn and understand. Take the matter as you have seen it. However, everything that is hot must one day become cool. In one's, life one could at times expect bad things to happen and as such, one should wear a heart of stone. One year can never be the end of ones life as it will some day come to pass. See your imprisonment period as a time for sober reflection, rehabilitation and reformation of your character for the better". Before Nelson's parents left Nelson, they promised to be visiting him from time to time. They gave Nelson two Dinab to enable him take care of himself at the prison.

Commenting on their way out of the prison; out of the sight of Nelson, Mr. Johnson Kenneth said to his wife "I am happy on the imprisonment which Nelson is serving now. That will act as a deterrent to him at this period and throughout his life time. People learn from history. Those that cannot learn from history are doomed. I am happy over the experiences which Nelson is having now. Nelson's life will be touched at least for having been denied his freedom which is very important and fundamental. It is bad for one who had eaten on the table to eat on the floor. But whoever touches a sleeping lion has invited trouble. On the part of Nelson's younger brothers and sisters at home, Nelson's condition of life now, will caution them to be of good behaviour at all cost. An intelligent person learns from what happened to another person. If what happened to Nelson has not happened, Nelson's style of life could have been worse and possibly would have brought disaster to our family through Nelson or through other children because as the cow chews the cud its young ones imitate it, bearing in mind that Nelson is the first child. What happened to Nelson could have happened to another child it is just a question of time".

CHAPTER FOURTEEN

On the part of Fabian, his parents expressed their displeasure over the poor state of his health when they surprisingly visited him at the prison. They felt so worried, Advising their son, Fabian's father, Mr. Thompson Daniel said "It was your poor behaviour that had made Fabian to be at this place. Exercise patience and take everything easy since the prison term will one day come to pass. Avail yourself of all the numerous opportunities aimed at rehabilitating, reforming and rebuilding prisoners. It is bad for one to go to the sea to bath but could not wash off the soap on one's body or go to the river only to get the container half filled with water. So make good use of available opportunities". He promised to be coming to see Fabian from time to time. Before they left Fabian, Fabian's parents gave their son one Dinab to enable him stay happily at the prison.

Nelson and Fabian stayed peacefully with the other inmates in the prison. They engaged in series of activities like the other inmates including begging for arms and in "fire baptism" exercise. It must be noted that Nelson and Fabian had become so hardened in heart with all the treatments they had received right from the time they were sent into the police cell. They had received severe tortures that had got them hardened in heart. They have not been exposed to such hard periods in their lives before the prison experience. With the carefree lives of most prison inmates, reckless smoking habits and notorious attitudes of most prison Inmates, Nelson and Fabian joined the wagon of terrible people.

The boys were engaged not only in the smoking of ordinary cigarettes as they were doing before but also in the smoking of hemp. Many prison inmates were hemp smokers and the boys There was no serious rehabilitation and reformation actually for prison inmates. What was obtainable at the prison was several sorts of moral decadence and decay.

Most of those who were assigned by the government to rehabilitate prison inmates had abandoned their assignments for other things which are non-human reformatory. Some embezzled money meant for the upkeep of prisoners. Some of them had resorted to other engagements which they deem more lucrative with prison funds leaving the prisoners alone to live a life themselves cannot live. Many of the prison inmates are hardened criminals who had inculcated crime and cultured their ideas of bad habits to other inmates.

At that juncture, Nelson and Fabian had started doing more bad things than they were doing before they were sent into the prison. The boys had learnt more on smoking, pilfering, stealing, how to abuse people, cheat and other social ills. Nelson and Fabian at a certain time could not fear the police and prison warders any longer.

At about three weeks of the boys stay at the prison, they were still serving their masters. At a time, Nelson's master was no longer giving Nelson gifts and items as he did when Nelson came to the prison new. He had started reducing food items and other gifts to Nelson. But Nelson on the other hand supported those things on his own and had started using his master's items, properties and even started eating his master's food and rendering poor services as well.

One day, Nelson's master asked him why he had resorted to taking his things more than necessary and more than he himself has been giving to him. Nelson said "most actions that people do are not deliberate. I have resorted to taking my master's things by force since I want to provide for myself the basic needs appropriately. What my master is giving me is not enough".

Nelson's master said "I caution you Nelson to be careful with those acts which you have resorted to. I warn you because

because if you continue with those habits, I will have no option than to order for brutality on you which is our republic's way of disciplining inmates. I cannot please anyone to displease myself. Remember, our republic runs a parliamentary and military government".

With all those instructions, Nelson still reduced the level of services he was rendering to his master. At a time, Nelson reduced services drastically to the extent that his master and others felt that reduction in service. One day, Nelson's master called on Nelson for a chat to find out why he had drastically reduced the services he was rendering to him. Nelson in his response said "I am sorry for the poor services envisaged in me. Under a normal situation when an employer pays his employees as if they are joking, the employees could render services to the employer as if they are joking".

That resulted into a poor state of relationship between Nelson and his master for a while. Even though both greeted each other, there wasn't any intimate relationship between them as before. That became noticeable among other prison inmates. Nelson was still serving but not as well as before.

At a time, Nelson realised his weak points that led to the poor relationship and wanted to reconcile with his master. One day, he went to his master but Nelson's master thinking that Nelson had come for a favour shouted at Nelson "have you come for gifts?" Nelson was infuriated, worried and annoyed. Nelson however ignored the statement and continued with his reconciliation bid. Talking to his master Nelson said "I am sorry for what had happened and for what I have failed to do. I was just giving out services exactly as I was receiving" His master commenting said "I will reverse to my kindness to you while Nelson should continue with his good services".

The boys at a certain time got used to the prison life. After about three months of the boys stay at the prison, the Secretary of their republic and his assistant finished their jail term and left the prison premises for their respective homes. Nelson and Fabian were given the post of Secretary and Assistant Secretary of the republic respectively. At the meeting in which the boys were given their portfolios, it was anunanimous decision electing the boys into those posts. The other inmates had considered the boys educated and capable of handling the posts and therefore allowed them to take up the positions.

It must be noted that news of Nelson's and Fabian's imprisonment had fast circulated throughout Lawson Grammar School and the boys villages too. News of bad things often spread faster than good news. At Nelson's village, Thorlando, an old woman who heard of Nelson's imprisonment said "I did not receive the news with surprise. Nelson's grandfather was carefree, naughty, arrogant and notorious when he was alive. Nelson is like his grandfather. The blood does not tell lies. Good and bad all lie in the blood. Also, Nelson was delivered after about seven months of his stay inside his mother's womb instead of the normal nine months making him an unusual human being. A person that will be good in character is noted when he or she is in the womb. The type of life, behaviour and attitude a person will portray during adulthood is noticed when the person is in the womb. Nelson should be advised to be of good behaviour and not be pompous and wasteful because of his father's riches; or see the whole world as a place that only him should occupy. The size of one is what one can occupy on a bench. The boy should not be carefree".

Later on, Nelson observed that he had lost weight and was deteriorating in appearance as a result of poor feeding and poor maintenance at the prison. One day, he complained to his master by saying "I am loosing weight and deteriorating in appearance as a result of poor feeding". Responding, Nelson's master said "hunger does not kill any one but rather makes one's eyes to swell and one's body to shrink". Nelson who burst into laughter later asked his master thus "can't one die if the person's eyes are swelling and the body shrinking? Nelson's master said "no". Nelson laughed the more.

After about four months of Nelson's and Fabian's stay at the prison, the prisoners were taken out of the prison for a parade. It was a leisure fare parade meant to expose prisoners to life outside the prison environment.

On the parade, Nelson and Fabian saw a man handling an expensive and fanciful briefcase. The boys signaled each other over the development. They left the parade ground and followed the man closely till a place where no one could see them and the man with the briefcase.

The boys having the impression that the briefcase could be containing valuables like money went up to the man and snatched the briefcase from the man and ran away to a far away place. Thereafter, the boys destroyed the briefcase and after a careful search of the briefcase they discovered to their utmost surprise that the briefcase was containing papers and not money. The boys felt highly disappointed and with annoyance ran back to the owner of the briefcase and got him terribly beaten up and after that left the place and the briefcase. That was to show that the boys had become hardened criminals.

CHAPTER FIFTEEN

While serving their jail term, the boys' parents were coming to see their wards. As the parents visited their children they brought to them wards food, clothes and money.

The boys however, adjusted to the life obtainable at the acclaimed republic however. They kept doing the routine activities done in the prison alongside with the other inmates.

Inmates who normally stay inside the prison at times wore mufty apart from the prison dresses. Nelson's parents have always noticed that. But each time Nelson's parents visited him, they had seen him always in the prison attire. One day, Nelson's mother asked Nelson why he had preferred prison attire to other dresses which they had brought to him. Nelson in his response said "the atmosphere in which I have found myself is such that does not give room for good dressing. I have been in a horrible situation, which I am not supposed to be and which does not accommodate good dressing. If one is relaxed and lives in a good environment and is happy, then the person can talk of dressing well and changing clothes that are worn-out. One good thing leads to another".

Flomy did not visit Nelson and Fabian at the prison either. She had quickly taken to friendship to Tom Noel a student at their school who happened to be Nelson and Fabian's friend. Tom Noel had asked Flomy once about Nelson and Fabian. In her response, Flomy said "I forgot all about Nelson and Fabian the day the boys were reported to have been imprisoned. I got into love with someone else to have someone to occupy my idle time, provide my needs and above all provide me with happiness and comfort. Normally, soldiers go, soldiers come; lovers go, lovers come, barrack remain the same".

Nelson and Fabian used to behave very well each time they see any prison worker. That was aimed at drawing sympathy from such worker. The boys will do as if they were good people. Such prison worker could give the boys a greater share of any item being distributed to prison inmates. When the boys must have received those lion share of any item being shared, they will laugh at the prison officer when the worker leaves their vicinity.

The boys were so much doing eye service. During work by prisoners, the boys will work conscientiously to the admiration of the prison officers. That was to attract sympathy from such officers. As a result of that, the boys were so much admired by the supervisors. But at situations where there are no officers, the boys may not work at all. Even if they work, they will work without concentration and seriousness

At that juncture, the boys could be reported to the authorities as doing their jobs poorly or not doing it at all. The authorities at such a state will not take such complaint serious. They will regard such complaint as a false accusation aimed at tarnishing the boys image. The boys believed in working hard on supervision to the admiration of the officers and doing the contrary when not supervised.

There came a day when Nelson and Fabian were taken out of the prison yard to the town by two prison warders for sight seeing and begging. The boys were on their prison attire during the outing. During the trip, Fabian saw a pretty lady and drew her attention by calling her. The lady seeing Fabian on a prison attire ran away. Fabian while trying to console himself said to Nelson "the lady is ugly, I made a mistake calling her".

Nelson did not buy Fabian's idea on the lady but rather said to Fabian "you are consoling yourself on the lady that shunned you and ran away. Prisoners are like photographers who while men and women are busy enjoying themselves in a soul and body party and touching themselves as well, are busy taking pictures of those in the party and cannot touch any of the fine ladies that their fellow men are romancing except by mistake. Photographers hardly get a piece of the earthly action. I cannot be a photographer no matter the circumstance", Fabian burst into laughter. That was the first time Fabian was having a good heart thrilling laugh since he came into the prison.

The prisoners conditions kept worsening due to poor maintenance. The situation deteriorated to the extent that worn-out prison dresses could not be replaced by the authorities. Bulks of the money sent by the government for the upkeep of prisoners were squandered by prison authorities among other people to the detriment of the prisoners. Nelson and Fabian suffered as a result of the prison authorities actions and inactions.

The prison then, which Nelson and Fabian were serving their jail term then was not for proper character reformation as was the mandate then. The bulk of the money meant to carter for the prisoners all round development and training then were diverted into private pockets and prisoners suffered. In fact, there was no genuine rehabilitation for the prisoners.

CHAPTER SIXTEEN

After about five months of Nelson's and Fabian's stay at the prison, "The Gatherers of Men Fellowship Association" (GMFA) visited the many prisoners at the prison where the boys were serving their jail term. Information of members of the association's visit was conveyed to inmates of the prison accordingly before the visit.

Members of the Association, a non-denominational christian association had come for evangelic work of preaching the gospel of God to the prison inmates. That was an assignment which the association had embarked upon to save mankind from moral collapse. The association was also a religious one on a moral reformatory exercise.

At the first day of the association's visit to the boys' prison, Nelson and Fabian did not attend to their preaching. The attendance was not compulsory, so not all the inmates were there. But the association came with assorted types of delicious food for the prison inmates. Those that attended to their call and gathering were highly entertained with foods, drinks, gifts and religious preaching.

The association's visit to the prison and preaching touched the lives of many prison inmates who quickly turned a new leaf after hearing heart thrilling and mind touching preachings. After that first day, members of the association promised to repeat their visit to the inmates in seven days time to know if the inmates had responded and appreciated their teachings.

When Nelson and Fabian heard of the high quality foods and drinks served by members of Gatherers of Men Fellowship Association to prison inmates at the first day of their visit, the boys felt highly annoyed over the food they missed. They nearly cried. They felt sorry for what they had failed to do. Each blamed the other for causing their failure to go for the foods. Fabian consoling himself before Nelson for what he had missed shouted in slangs thus "do not mind those guys fucking up and raping shit".

The boys waited patiently for the day the association planned a rescheduled visit. On the rescheduled day, members of the association visited the inmate as promised. Nelson and Fabian wanted to eat food quite unobtainable at the prison and as such came to the venue of the gathering before schedule time waiting. Before the association started with the assignments for that day, the members first served the skeletal and hungry prisoners good food. That was to bring the body and soul of the inmates together as it is believed that "a hungry man is an angry man." Nelson and Fabian wanted to leave the place after being treated with the good dishes but later withheld the idea. Fabian told Nelson "let us exercise a little patience so that we could at least hear a bit of the message which the association had brought to us. It is wise for us to reciprocate the good food we have eaten by at least listening to the message which the association had come with. If we do not stay a little while, it would be as if we are hungry people that have come out for food." So, the boys stayed.

Then came the real activities. The leader of the association kicked off the programmes of the day by a with heart touching prayers. After the prayers the leader of the group said, "It is the devil that makes people get imprisoned. That is possible because the devil in the inmates had occupied the heart of the inmates thereby making God to have a little portion in their hearts to direct their good course. The dance, the movie, worldly songs, worldly clothing, earthly houses, cars and uneternal company are only bubbles on the stream of time that will one day come to pass. There is no place like heaven. Diseases, sicknesses and prison are of the devil not of God. There is no evil in heaven. Change for the better. It is not late. It is only when one works hard, behave well and forget about all uselessnesses that one can enter into heaven where one can only enjoy life of abundance till eternity. Start a good life today before it becomes late. Start off this project of making heaven today and build it gradually till you realise that goal. Rome was not built in a day. A project started must one day be completed. It is just a question of time".

Some other members of the association male and female preached too. They played their religious live band for so long and sang heart touching songs of praises to God. What touched Nelson and Fabian most and made them to change on that spot was the young people in the group who were seen happy and healthy and were preaching the gospel and dancing and rejoicing to praise God, while they (Nelson and Fabian) were wasting in the prison. Some of those people were younger than Nelson and Fabian. That contributed in making the boys to think twice and rightly.

At the night, members of the association projected religious films for prison inmates.

With the series of programmes the association held for prison inmates, some prisoners repented and changed their ways of life for the better. After the night's film shows, members of the association departed. In fact, the impact of the association's visit at the prison was great and memorable and had a lot of things to tell on the lives of many prisoners.

On the part of Nelson and Fabian, their lives had changed for the better. They repented and promised to give their lives to God and to God's services. They promised to give up bad acts and be of good behaviour throughout their lives. Nelson resolved to join the Association and serve God till he dies. In fact, the boys have changed. The boys were highly touched morally. That was "a great turn around".

Right at the prison, where the boys were kept, they started preaching the word of God to other prison inmates who have not repented. They were many times seen praying and singing christian songs. Nelson and Fabian had wondered why they came into the prison. They realised that they had erred. They wished that what happened to bring them into the prison had not happened at all. They wished the term of their imprisonment had finished so that they could go into the world to live a good life and preach the gospel of God.

CHAPTER SEVENTEEN

Two weeks after the members Of Gatherers of Men Fellowship Association's "Operation storm the devil" programme, the Chief Judge of Tomnor State visited prison inmates in Shotaran prison. The visit of the Chief Judge was aimed at finding out the problems prisoners were encountering at their prisons with the aim of improving on their living condition. Secondly, it was to release some prisoners whose terms of imprisonment were almost completed or remaining less than a year. It was also aimed at releasing some prisoners whose offences were minor and could be pardoned ordinarily, it was also to release prisoners whose health condition is in terrible condition And finally, it was to release inmates who would have completed their tenure if they were convicted of their offences but had stayed longer than that in the prison. There was prison congestion in the state then.

When the Chief Judge of the state visited the prison, the prison authorities assembled all the prison inmates at the prison field for an address by the State Chief Judge, Honourable Justice Joel Brown. Addressing the prisoners, the Chief Judge said "I lament on the rising state of crime and juvenile delinquency in the state. No meaningful government can afford to see her subjects waste or suffer in misery and penury. I advise you prisoners to be of immense use to yourselves in order to be useful to your communities and entire society. Even though the economy has been mismanaged by the rulers that is not a reason for people to take to illicit activities to earn a living. It is not the issue of the mismanagement of an economy that matters but the ability of the inhabitants to adjust their lives to suit that economy in place through hardwork, avoidance of ostentatious living, wasteful spending and frivolities. A revolution to deal with economic saboteurs is better than social ills by people. The rulers of any society or place determine the state of the economy and other things. If the rulers want it to be good, a good economy comes into being. If the rulers want it to be bad, a poor state of an economy comes to stay. The rulers has the knife and the yam and apportions to anyone or to the society according to their wish. I advise you prison inmates not to engage in crime because if ones reputation is lost everything is lost. Once an individual's reputation is brought to question, dignity, integrity and acceptance are all lost. Engage in meaningful activities which will be to your benefits and to the overall welfare of the society. The lives you live will tell on you so much on the later parts of your lives. If you work hard at your youth, that will be to your advantage in your old age. The type of seed one plants to a great extent determines the type of crop or fruit the person will reap later. Keep-off bad companies that could lead you astray. The state is ready to assist any of her indigenes who tries to help himself or herself. But the State will first investigate into the job or services one is engaging before coming to the person's assistance".

The Chief Judge paused for a while before he said thus, "ordinarily, one will ask how well an individual is doing before assisting the concerned person. Please, shun the craze for materialism as that could lead you into crime. Money is not everything. Money is not long life, good health, happiness and therefore not everything. The society will continue to recognize and appreciate good things and shun bad things. People who engage in good deeds must continue to have their names written in gold while those that do evil must always find themselves in unpleasant and uncomfortable situations. Whoever that is doing something good may it work out well for the person and whoever is planning evil may the person not succeed in this our state. Most people who are imprisoned received their troubles because they had cheated the government and had treated the government in isolation. Whoever has taken part in running down a system which the person is part of has not done any meaningful act at all. A snake that has swallowed its young one has taken in what it has given out and therefore has not done much".

Furthermore, the Chief Judge asked the prison inmates thus, "do you know that our rulers messed up the economy and brought untold hardship to the citizens". Some of those skeletal looking prison inmates replying said "yes". Honourable Justice Brown talking to the prison inmates again said "1 do not pity prominent people that die mysteriously for most of such people commit atrocities to get to their privileged positions. Here on earth, they are paid according to their misdeeds. It is just a question of time, but it must happen. It is not as if I am antagonizing the rulers personally or that I have much against them, the issue is that one must say bad of evils. Even though the rulers can be good to those in authority their goodness is not real goodness at all. Theymake things too hard for people that their favours make no meaning really to anyone since their gifts have little or no value. When a favour outweighs its costs such cannot be counted as a favour any longer. If I have a way I should have killed some of them for long for life is not fit for them. It is better for some people to die than for the masses to perish. Not all deaths are natural for hunger and diseases kill people with poverty. People who would not have died with good care die with hardship. A society is corrupt because the leaders are corrupt. It is the type of leadership style that leaders exhibit that subjects follow. When the cattle chews the cud their young ones imitate them. When a system is bad at the top all the systems could be bad till the end; no two ways about it. Bad leaders could be worse than the devil for the devil could accommodate its fellow devils and possibly have conscience but bad leaders don't have conscience. Bad rulers are devils in the form of human beings. No nation can suffer untold hardship with good leadership. Nations suffer severely as a result of had leadership. People suffer in nations not because of lack of resources but due to corruption brought in state by bad leaders.

Every society that is corrupt must suffer even with abundance of resources; man and material. Nations are in huge debts with absolutely nothing to show for it due to misrule. For Loans meant for work were diverted into private pockets. Bad rulers most of the time fortify their security to save themselves from attack from those they offend unlike good leaders. So there is need for human beings to be good for posterity and for the good of all. With good people and good leadership there will be prosperity, peace, unity and love. With good people and good leadership many of those in prison at any point in time may not find themselves in that pitiable condition. So anywhere you find yourselves be good for the benefit of all".

The Chief Judge paused for a while before he said "I have granted pardon to all prisoners whose jail term is remaining less than a year. All prisoners who are jailed for minor offences like fighting, pilfering among others will be set free. Prisoners whom their health conditions are poor will be set free. All those who have been in prison longer than would have been the case if they are convicted of their offence will be set free".

At that juncture, one of the prisoners said to the Chief Judge "I am a chain smoker and a hardened criminal; I have in addition to what I know before being sent into the prison learnt a lot of terrible things here in the prison. I have just spent only ten days in the prison but can at moment punch someone at a particular place and kill the person immediately, which I did not know before I came into the prison. In fact, I have learnt so many evils here in the prison. Please release me for the better as my continued stay in the prison cannot be to the society's benefit". The man brought out from his pocket a wrapped stick of Indian hemp and showed it to the Chief Judge. He lit the Indian hemp with a match from his pocket and smoked it before the Chief Judge. He further posed before the Chief Judge his hand muscles.

In his response, the Chief Judge directed that the prisoner should be released alongside with the other categories of prisoners who were to be freed. Most of those prisoners who were to be freed thanked the Chief Judge for his kindness and magnanimity. Many of them promised the Chief Judge that they will turn a new leaf and be of a high state of responsibility and usefulness.

It is remarkable to note that soon after the Chief Judge's visit to the prison, a top government functionary died, some days after. His corpse was buried after staying two months in the mortuary. His corpse was buried at a government cemetery. A day after the burial, an angry mob raided the cemetery, overpowered the security men guarding the place, removed the corpse from the expensive coffin it was buried and vandalized the coffin leaving the corpse without any coffin.

A day after the incident, another mob raided the same cemetery and flogged the corpse. It was alleged that the corpse was flogged more than five hundred strokes of the cane.

Two days after, another angry mob raided the same cemetery and the security men on duty guiding the place helped the mob in burning the corpse. All that was to show annoyance over bad leadership then. It seemed as if a revolution had started as people took the laws into their hands; as the Chief Judge wanted.

CHAPTER EIGHTEEN

On the part of the prison authorities, they did not allow those prisoners who were freed to go home that day. They promised those to be freed that they will compile their names, and prepare the necessary documentations necessary for their release and departure. The prison authorities promised to finish the assignments the following morning to enable all those freed to go.

The following morning, all those who were freed had packed for their departure. Before eight o'clock that morning the prison autholities had compiled the names of all those who were to go. All those who were to go had already assembled at the prison reception awaiting the gates of the prison to be opened for them. As the Controller of the prison called the names of those who had been freed, there was jubilation from different angles that day. As the names of those concerned were called, other inmates shouted the name or nicknames (if any) which that person was known in the prison. Most of those freed had one nickname of the other. Each person called was given some money to enable the person pay transport fare home.

Nelson and Fabian were called simultaneously. The boys carried their bags, collected their transport money, acknowledged cheers from other inmates and left the prison. Nelson and Fabian had nicknames in prison before they repented. Their nick names were Pupee and Chunky respectively. The boys ignored their nicknames, saluted the other inmates and the prison authorities and left. Some of the prison workers that loved the boys escorted them to a place where the boys boarded a vehicle.

Nelson and Fabian boarded a taxi and returned to their respective homes. At their homes, it was jubilation all over; to welcome them. Nelson's parents were surprised to see their son at their home when it was not yet time for him to complete his jail term. Nelson's parents, brothers and sisters rejoiced greatly when they saw Nelson alive, healthy and lively.

After about an hour of Nelson's return to his home, Nelson called on members of his family and narrated to them his recent experiences at the prison, how he was released, what he had learnt in the prison and how he had been converted to a devoted Christian. Nelson started preaching to the admiration of all listening to him. He informed all those listening to him that everything under the sun is vanity and will all end up here on earth never extending to heaven. In their response, members of Nelson's family expressed happiness over what the Chief Judge did.

Nelson did not stop at his family with his gospel preaching. He kept preaching from house to house around his home. Some people who heard Nelson and his preaching believed in what he was saying while some did not believe. One man who heard Nelson and his preaching said to Nelson "It is not the issue of people saying bad of someone that matter in life but the ability of the mouth that had said bad to change and say good in the life style and behavior of the person whom bad had been said of before that matters. It is a good thing for the mouth that had said bad about Nelson to turn around to say good of that same person". However, some people who heard Nelson preaching believed him while some did not; wondering whether he had been possessed by demon.

At home Nelson's parents tried to know whether he has actually turned a new leaf or not. They gave Nelson a huge sum of money to keep for them. Nelson kept the money and brought it out when he was asked to bring the money. He did not tamper with it. That made his parents believe that he has actually become a very good person.

However, some people believed him, some could not, stating that such could be a gimmick aimed at having an opportunity to do worse.

Fabian's family members, relatives, friends and well- wishers were very happy to see a new Fabian who is responsible, reasonable and who is also preaching the gospel of God. However, some people did not believe that.

Also, Fabian's parents tried to know whether he has actually repented or not. They did that by giving him a huge sum of money to buy a plastic bucket for them. The money given to Fabian was about ten times the price of the bucket. Fabian's parents wanted to know whether Fabian will take the balance of the money after purchasing the bucket.

But after buying the bucket, Fabian gave his parents the balance of the money. That proved to Fabian's parents that he has actually changed for good.

At Fabian's home, the story was the same. Fabian's people expressed happiness over the Chief Judge's mercy on their son. The parents of Nelson and Fabian after about three days of the boys' return wrote to the Chief Judge expressing happiness over the Chief Judge's gesture.

After about two weeks of the boys stay at their respective homes, their parents thought of how to assist and make the boys lives meaningful again. They had seen the boys as repentants who were highly desirous for a better future.

After some close door discussions with the boys, the parents of Nelson and Fabian found out that the boys were highly interested in acquiring education. The boys had repented and had apologized for what they had done and for what they had failed to do in the past.

On the part of Nelson, he had chosen to go into the seminary to serve God and mankind. Fabian did not sanction the idea of going into the seminary but promised to live a modest, ideal, useful and meaningful life throughout his existence on earth.

Fabian's parents took him to Lawson Grammar School for re-admission. When Fabian was seen at the school by his fellow students who had known him before, they surrounded him and hailed him by his former name of Yob Fab, which was Fabian's nickname at the school before he was imprisoned. Some of them had expected to see a worse Fabian but to their greatest surprise, they saw a better Fabian. Not only seeing a better Fabian, they saw Fabian of good life and modesty. Some students and staff of the school could not believe what they were seeing. But some believed.

The Principal refused re-admitting Fabian that time but later reconsidered his decision and re-admitting Fabian on trial. A letter of undertaking signed and counter-signed by Fabian and his father indicated that the former would be of good behaviour throughout his stay at the school. They signed that any act short of that will earn Fabian severe disciplinary action or outright dismissal as the case may be.

Fabian was then re-admitted into Lawson Grammar School. He packed to the school the following day and started studies. At the school, Fabian did not compromise anything for his studies. He participated in so many religious activities in the school. In fact, the Fabian before his jail term was not the same Fabian after his freedom. That was envisaged in Fabian's acts, utterances, associations, manners and academic works.

In the academic aspect, Fabian repeated the second year which he was in before he was imprisoned. He was a symbol of excellence in the school academically, morally, physically and mentally. He did not get any position less than the fourth in the class in all examinations. He won prizes in academics; moral excellence and in socials. Fabian helped many students to become of good behaviour too. He tried much in preaching to other students particularly those whom he knew to be of the same behaviour like him before he was jailed.

At their school some ladies tried to fumble with Fabian by trying to have a love making relationship with him to know whether he has actually repented or not but Fabian ignored them and rather preached Christianity to them.

CHAPTER NINETEEN

On the part of Nelson, he sought admission into a Seminary College. He succeeded. He was offered admission at Saint Patrick Seminary College, Fortland. At the seminary, Nelson found out that the place was actually where he belong. It is said that "whatever is meant to work out will surely succeed no matter the circumstances that could be envisaged". Nelson did exceptionally well at the school. In academics, morals, mental alertness and reasoning, Nelson Kenneth was a name to be reckoned with at the school.

Nelson visited Lawson Grammar School so many times at his stay at Saint Patrick Seminary College and preached the gospel of the Lord to the students and staff of the school. Nelson centred his preaching mostly on those students he knew were of bad behaviour during the time he himself was at the school and was of poor behaviour.

At Fabian's forth year in his school, he contested election to be the compound prefect of his school. Fabian had seen the environment of his school deteriorating in cleanliness and standard. He wanted to pick up the compound perfectship of the school to sanitize the system. Some students did not want to vote for him with the assumption that Fabian was still a bad student who was pretending to be a good one.

Even though Fabian on his own helped in cleaning the school premises at his own time, some students still thought that Fabian was a wolf in a sheep's clothing. Some of the students did not take Fabian serious, even with all his good actions. Those students believed that genuine character change on the part of Fabian is not possible as his mind may be completely rotten and cannot be amended. They never knew that things could be changed with time. However, Fabian defeated his opponent. Many students who voted for him did so because they wanted to give Fabian a trial to find out whether he was a good person or not.

Fabian won the election with a small margin. During his tenure of office as the Compound Prefect of Lawson Grammar School, Fabian did exceptionally well that the students and staff of the school recognized and appreciated his efforts and ingenuity. They wished Fabian could continue after his tenure of office. Many staff and students begged Fabian to go for a second term but Fabian refused.

Flomy tried to reach out to Nelson as a lover but Nelson refused such relationship. He accepted the girl as a mere friend. The boy had changed and had discarded such acts with ladies totally what more with Flomy who did not even visit them at their troubled times in the prison. The boy rather kept on preaching to Flomy to change and turn over a new leaf. But Flomy kept to her old type of life of juvenile delinquency. Nelson tried all he could to make Flomy change for the better but his efforts did not yield fruitful results.

Throughout the period Nelson was in the seminary, he was a good person. There was no bad thing that was associated with him at all. Nelson participated actively in many religious activities. He even introduced some religious programmes in that seminary which both the seminary authorities and fellow seminarians appreciated and enshrined into the seminary's programmes. Nelson was determined to achieve more successes after his career in the seminary having the belief that "it is where one assignment terminates that another starts". Nelson was in fact a force to be reckoned with at the seminary.

There were some statements that the Rector of the seminary made which Nelson centred his mind on in whatever he did. The Rector, Reverend Smith Hill always told his students that "the successes that could be attributed to one in life are dependent on what that person achieves at a particular day". The Rector always told his boys that "one should aim at achieving greatness through hard work, patience and dedication." He always told the seminarians that "the minor successes that one records on a daily basis when joined together forms a bundle of achievements." He told his boys, never to spare any success as when each is overlooked the overall success of that individual is adversely effected. He equally told his students that the body is so weak, does not like to work, likes to rest and that people should not allow their body to control their senses but rather allow their senses to control their body. The Rector always told them that Rome was not built in a day but over a great number of years. He told them to aspire to build greatness in their lifetime for posterity and possibly have their names immortalized for life with good. He kept informing students that one cannot be judged by the number of opportunities one has but by the usefulness one makes out with the opportunities given to one. He even said that where one runs to another can trek to that place.

Experience is the best teacher so people say. Nelson have had the experience in what good and bad manners are and could bring to someone. He was therefore in a better position to understand and appreciate what the Rector was saying. In addition, he was at various times counseling people. He has found rest in God, obtained salvation and had found the usefulness of good behaviour. He had known that "those who cannot learn from history may be doomed for life".

CHAPTER TWENTY

Fabian and Nelson maintained a friendly relationship during their school days and in fact throughout their lifetime. While they were in their respective schools they corresponded and visited each other so often. They loved each other so much. Their friendship at a time became such that they became inseparable. They were like tea and sugar that can hardly be separated. They have a lot of things in common and acted like brothers. They have shared similar experiences in the past.

Fabian completed his studies in Lawson Grammar School. He did very well at the final examinations. He also gained admission that year at Norman University to read Law.

Nelson completed his studies the following year and was sent to Britain for further studies in theology by Saint Patrick Seminary College

Fabian read Law at Norman University. He did exceptionally well at the University. He made a first class degree in Law. That was a rare grade in that course in the university. He has been with his good manners and excellent conduct. He was after his studies at the Law school called to the bar.

On the part of Nelson, he read theology at Renewal Institute of Theology in Britain. He obtained his Bachelor of Arts in Theology after five years of studies at the Institute. He made a first class Honours degree in Theology. He was thereafter ordained a Protestant Priest. That was historic.

Like some other students, Flomy did not change for the better morally initially but she did later however. Flomy's change for a good moral disposition was due to the handiwork of Nelson, who continuously preached and counseled her to change for the better. As a result of Flomy's change for the better she got engaged to Nelson and eventually got married to him.

Nelson continued with his good manners, excellent conduct and hardwork. After Nelson's studies at Renewal Institute of Theology, the institute retained him to teach at the institution. During his second year of lecturing and studies at the institute, he obtained his Masters of Arts Degree Certificate(MA) in theology from the institute. Nelson lectured at the institute afterwards. During that period of Nelson's studies and teaching at the Renewal Institute of Theology, Barrister Fabian Daniel and his wife visited Nelson at Britain. At the airport to receive Fabian where Nelson, his wife, friends, students, staff of his Institute among others. Fabian and his wife stayed with Nelson in Britain for two weeks before returning to his country. It was a historic and pleasant trip for Fabian and his wife.

Both Pastor Nelson Kenneth and Barrister Fabian Daniel made great impact in their country. They contributed in the growth and development of their country and in the world at large. They were prominent, highly respected and influential people. That was the great impact which was contrary to the expectation of many who witnessed when the concerned people derailed.